OUTSIDE EDEN

BOOKS BY ISABEL SCOTT RORICK

MR. AND MRS. CUGAT

OUTSIDE EDEN

isabel scott rorick

OUTSIDE EDEN

drawings by constantin alajalov

HOUGHTON MIFFLIN COMPANY BOSTON 1945

The Riverside Press Cambridge

The Riverside Press
CAMBRIDGE · MASSACHUSETTS
PRINTED IN THE U.S.A.

TO C. H. R. AGAIN

GRATEFUL ACKNOWLEDGMENTS ARE MADE TO
'COLLIER'S MAGAZINE' AND TO THE 'JUNIOR
LEAGUE MAGAZINE' FOR PERMISSION TO
USE SOME OF THE MATERIAL IN THIS BOOK.

CONTENTS

1

REMEMBER THE SABBATH

Some men are what is known as 'handy around the house.' They can, if need be, fix a dripping faucet, plane off a door that sticks, put up a hook in the back hall or paint the cellar steps. The craftsmen of the genus have workshops in their basements, expensively equipped, and will turn out, in their spare time, an occasional end-table for the living-room or furniture for the yard. The dreamers, touched with genius, will devote whole lives to model planes or trains — or ships in bottles. Mr. Cugat, though, was none of these.

He was a good provider — sober and industrious, well-thought-of in financial circles for sagacity and acumen, an excellent bridge player and a natural athlete, but he was about as handy as a seal in mittens. Mr. Cugat had been spared, however, any realization of this. His confidence in himself was modest but sublime. In spite of the fact that the base plugs he investigated blew the main fuse, doorknobs he tightened came off in his hand, plaster cracked, glass shattered, nails bent double, paint formed puddles, and he always cut himself, he was wont to say offhandedly that he must get around to fixing this or that some of these days so as to 'get it done right for once.' Fortunately for everybody concerned, the jobbing department of a contracting firm by the name of B. Allerton and Sons Company, at the urgent behest of Mrs. Cugat, generally got around first and, at a price, put things to rights before they could again come to his notice.

1

But one night after dinner he said in a businesslike tone, 'I want to look at the basement.'

'What for?' asked Mrs. Cugat uneasily.

'Well, I bought a little wine today. I've decided to lay some away. Start a cellar. The imported stuff is about gone, so I thought I'd buy some while I could, and I want to see where's the best place to keep it.'

'Oh,' she said, relieved. The hot-water heater had been acting up again and she was afraid he'd decided to look into it. The last time he'd looked into the hot-water heater he'd had to go around for a month without any eyebrows. 'There's the fruit room,' she said hesitantly, leading the way down the stairs.

The fruit room, however, not unnaturally, appeared to be full of fruit. But clear it out and it was just what he needed. Yes, siree! A narrow strip of wood could be nailed along the back of the shelves and another along the front so that the bottles could be tipped, and it was dark and cool. He began making enthusiastic plans.

'But where will we put the jelly?' protested Mrs. Cugat. 'There aren't any shelves anywhere else and Anna and I planned to put up more than ever this year.'

'Oh, we can build a few shelves somewhere else for that,' said Mr. Cugat easily. 'There's plenty of room in the laundry.'

'Well, all right,' she acceded doubtfully, 'I'll call Allerton's in the morning, then.'

'Allerton's!' he expostulated, shocked. 'Do you happen to know, young lady, how much you have to pay a carpenter, per hour, these days?'

Mrs. Cugat, of course, did not. Neither did Mr. Cugat, when pinned down, but anyway, it was universally known to be an exorbitant wage and like throwing money into the street to call one in for just a few shelves. He'd put up a few shelves for her and her jellies — some Sunday after golf. Order up the lumber tomorrow, he said indulgently, and he'd do it this Sunday! Mrs. Cugat attempted tactful dissuasion, but he'd begun to like the idea. Very well, leave it to him, then, he'd order the lumber himself, the first thing in the morning. He had a customer, as a matter of fact, who could probably get it for him wholesale. Was there some kind of rule around? He'd just take the necessary measurements.

Mrs. Cugat, somewhat impressed, produced the tape measure from her knitting bag and he repaired, whistling, to the laundry to stretch it professionally here and there, eyes narrowed.

Mrs. Cugat's tape measure may have been to blame or maybe the obliging customer was simply overgenerous, but the truckload of lumber that rolled into the yard the next afternoon looked like a lot. Mrs. Cugat, anxiously, from a window, watched while three men took just under an hour to unload it — mostly on the vegetable garden. Anna exclaimed with interest. A new back porch? She'd been wanting to say something for a long time. Summer nights the kitchen got so hot she'd been near to fainting. Hastily dashing this hope before it could develop the proportions of a grievance, Mrs. Cugat said no, Mr. Cugat was just planning to put up a few shelves in the laundry so they could use the fruit room for something else. Anna looked blank. Where was the laundry to be done, then? Did Mrs. Cugat realize they were washing curtains this week? Them carpenters and their dirty feet!

'You won't be bothered by any carpenters, Anna,' Mrs. Cugat said with dignity. 'Mr. Cugat's going to put up the shelves himself.'

'The *mister?*'

'Yes,' she said lightly and avoided Anna's eye.

Home from the office, that evening, Mr. Cugat was to be seen from the back windows regarding the pile of lumber

3

soberly. When he came into the house, however, his tone was casual. 'Must have made my measurements a bit generous,' he observed, 'but no harm done. It's not a bad idea to have some spare lumber on hand these days, it's pretty hard to get.'

'But where will we keep it?' she asked anxiously.

He sighed, suddenly weary. 'Don't ask me to figure out anything tonight!' he exclaimed. 'What a day! I haven't had five minutes to catch my breath.'

'You're going to carry it in soon, though, aren't you?' she pursued, nevertheless. 'It's ruining the grass.'

'I'll carry it in,' he said patiently, 'but I don't have to do it before dinner, do I?'

Dusk finally fell, blotting the raw pile from sight and mind and Mr. Cugat dozed peacefully in his chair. The next day he had to go to Washington.

Mr. Cugat was having to go to Washington more and more often of late, and frankly, Mrs. Cugat was getting good and sick of it. At first she had been excited and proud to think of him down there at the helm, helping to make history, conferring with the great, but Mr. Cugat had quickly pricked that pretty bubble. 'Any conferring I do is strictly with the hired help,' he informed her flatly.

'But you and Mr. Atterbury must meet *some* famous people,' she protested.

'Not in waiting-rooms,' he muttered.

'I mean,' she explained patiently, 'after you get in to see the man you've been waiting for.'

'We don't get in,' he said in a disgusted voice.

'*Never?*'

'Never.'

Mrs. Cugat was indignant. Mr. Cugat was a brilliant tax man — everybody said so! That men of his calibre were being made to waste their time sitting around in waiting-rooms was disgraceful. No wonder things were in a mess. Something

4

ought to be done. It made her mad every time she thought about it! Lying awake and thinking about it, in her lonely bedroom, on the nights he was gone, she calmed herself by fashioning dreamy palliatives — something she was very good at. Mr. Cugat, finally, coming to the attention of Morgenthau, would be asked to take charge of a difficult tax problem that nobody else could figure out and he would handle it so brilliantly that he would be appointed to a perfectly marvellous position, even though he was a Republican, and they would have to move to Washington for the duration, where they would have an apartment at the Carleton and meet simply everybody — like Lord Louis Mountbatten and Bob Hope and Madame Chiang Kai-shek. Here, Mrs. Cugat, finding it necessary to digress at some length to plan what she would wear for this happy occasion and to dwell on the envy that would surely gnaw at the breast of her good friend, Mrs. Sturm, would usually drift into such a pleasant mood that she'd drop off to sleep without further ado. Which was just as well, for she needed her sleep; the little burdens of everyday living seemed to weigh twice as much when borne alone. And now all this lumber piled up in the yard!

'Well, well! What are we building — a new wing?' called nextdoor neighbor, Mr. Cressey, jocularly over the rosebushes on Monday evening.

'Just a few shelves for the cellar,' she called back.

Mr. Cressey's eyebrows raised politely. 'My!' he said. 'Planning on *quite* a few, eh?'

It seemed, somehow, disloyal to shout, for all to hear, that Mr. Cugat had just made a mistake in his measurements, so she let it go by simply nodding brightly.

Mr. Cressey eyed the lumber enviously. 'I've been trying to get some material for a new garage for six months, but they say they haven't got it. I wish I knew how George talked them out of all that.'

5

'I'm afraid he got a little eloquent,' said Mrs. Cugat ruefully.

'Aggie, Cugits got a little elephant,' announced old Mr. Keubler across the street to his daughter-in-law. Mr. Keubler was ninety-one, vastly interested in everything and not as deaf as he might have been. Aggie emerged onto the porch.

'Maw!' bawled a young voice, not five seconds later, 'Cugats got a *baby elephant!*' One of the Louderback children, thought Mrs. Cugat, her heart sinking. The Louderback children were a large and virulent brood who jeered continually and on principle. Anna reported that the Louderbacks considered the Cugats stuck-up. Mrs. Cugat was scared to death of them.

'How chi-chi,' a sardonic adult voice replied. 'I always knew they were crazy.'

Pink and very stuck-up, Mrs. Cugat retired to the house and endeavored to put the whole thing out of her mind.

But on Tuesday noon, in the middle of lunch, the doorbell rang. Anna put down the dried beef and departed to answer it. Fork poised and inexplicably uneasy, Mrs. Cugat cocked her ears. There were questions and answers and a closing of doors.

'What is it?' she asked anxiously, as Anna reappeared in the dining-room door.

'Mr. Ernest Hemingway to see you,' Anna announced primly. 'I put him in the library.'

Mrs. Cugat sighed. 'I think you must have the name wrong, Anna,' she said gently. 'What did he say he wanted?'

'He wants to see you,' Anna explained patiently. 'He's one of them — you know — writer fellas.'

Mrs. Cugat, holding firmly to reason, put down her fork. 'Are you sure, Anna?'

'Yessum.'

She almost faltered at the library door, but managed to steel herself and turn the knob.

6

'Mrs. Cugat?' inquired a very young man with a snub nose and a crew haircut. Mrs. Cugat nodded blankly. 'I'm from the *Morning Spy*,' he said, swallowing. 'I'd like to get a story on your — ah — baby elephant.'

Mrs. Cugat explained gently.

'You mean you haven't — got one?' he stammered, looking ready to cry.

'I'm afraid not,' she apologized. 'It's just one of those silly things that got started —'

Mr. Hemingway rose violently to his feet, ran his fingers through what there was of his hair, walked over to the window and stood looking out, his legs spread, his back hunched. Mrs. Cugat was distressed. It seemed to mean a good deal to him.

He turned the face of a haggard baby. 'I've got to get a story,' he bit out. 'I've got to make good!' And then, in a more normal tone, added, 'This is my first assignment.'

Mrs. Cugat said she was *so* sorry, but what could she do?

'Nothing, of course,' he replied in dignified despair and turned back to the window.

After a minute or so she cleared her throat tentatively.

'Look,' he said abruptly, turning around again, 'what *are* you going to build out of all that timber?'

Mrs. Cugat sighed and embarked again upon the explanation of the shelves, but was brought up short by a terrified scream from somewhere outside, followed by what sounded like the cascading rumble of an avalanche. They dashed to the porch. Anna came running around the side of the house.

'Come quick!' she panted. 'One of them Louderback brats has got buried beneath our boards!'

Mr. Hemingway vaulted over the railing and Mrs. Cugat made for the steps.

In the side yard, the once neat, though towering, stack of lumber sprawled like a heap of jackstraws. From its depths came a faint whimper.

'There was one of 'em on top,' gabbled Anna, 'and one layin' down on the grass. When it started to go, the top one jumped, but the other never had a chance!'

Mr. Hemingway tore off his coat and they set frenziedly to work. It was only a matter of moments, really, before a somewhat flattened but apparently unhurt Louderback was brought to light, but it seemed like an eon.

'When my mother hears about this,' it said disagreeably, 'she's goin' to be *plenty* sore!'

Mrs. Cugat, Mr. Hemingway, and Anna sank to the back steps without breath to answer.

Mr. Hemingway recovered first. He walked over to his coat, put it on, and extracted from a pocket a notebook and pencil.

'What's your name and age?' he asked Anna in a suddenly businesslike tone. Anna obliged him meekly. 'Yours?' he said, turning to Mrs. Cugat. Mrs. Cugat, absorbed in picking the slivers out of her hand, replied abstractedly. 'Boy! What a scoop!' he beamed.

'Look,' said Mrs. Cugat slowly, 'What did you say *your* name was?'

'Harvey E. Hemingway — E for Ernest. Quite a coincidence, isn't it? I mean us both being writers. Oddly enough,' he added modestly, 'our styles are not unlike.' He turned to go and waved a hand. 'Well, be seeing you in the papers!'

It wasn't until fright had subsided and she began again to function normally that she started to worry about Mr. Hemingway's scoop. But by then it was a little late.

LOCAL SOCIALITE RESCUES TOT, the *Morning Spy* announced next day in a large box on the front page.

Sonny Louderback, 7, son of Mr. and Mrs. Lester P. Louderback, was saved from death yesterday by Mrs. Mary Elizabeth Cugat, 29, Junior League member and wife of the prominent banker, George B. Cugat, of 202 Huntington Drive. Buried beneath several hundred feet of heavy lumber, intended, it was said, for the construction of a shelter for a pet elephant, the lad was rescued only in the nick of time by the heroic efforts of the ninety-pound blueblood, who, with no thought for herself, toiled unceasingly to extricate him, administered First Aid and then collapsed. 'Anyone would have done the same,' she is quoted as saying.

By noon no less than a dozen persons had arrived to have a look at the lumber and the elephant — several with cameras. Anna spent a happy hour posing. By afternoon, no less than two dozen had arrived and Sonny Louderback was selling lemonade. A little man with a pony put in an appearance and began selling ten-cent rides around the yard. Beset, Mrs. Cugat called Allerton's and for six dollars and thirty-two cents, had the lumber carried out of sight behind the garage.

Mr. Cugat, back once again from the waiting-rooms of Washington, was highly amused. He also seemed rather relieved to find the lumber out of his sight for a while, even at that price. Lord, he was tired! Washington was a madhouse!

Then his wine came and, reviving, he carried it downstairs and unpacked it with enthusiasm all over the laundry floor. Sunday came and went.

'Darling, you seem to be so busy just now, don't you want me to call Allerton's again and have them come and finish up those shelves?' Mrs. Cugat urged tactfully.

Whether by accident or design, the laundress had kicked over one bottle and it had splashed liberally — on the clean laundry. Burgundy.

'Hell, *no*, honey,' he protested earnestly. 'Won't you ever get it into your little head that we've got to start saving money? With taxes what they are —'

But she cut him short. 'Will you get at the shelves pretty soon yourself, then? *This* Sunday, maybe? It's terribly inconvenient —'

Mr. Cugat promised that he would.

9

Sunday morning arrived and Cory Cartwright called to fix up the usual foursome, but Mrs. Cugat, on the alert, forestalled him.

'George can't play golf today, Cory,' she said firmly. 'He's going to put up some shelves in the basement.'

'He's going to do what?' exclaimed Mr. Cugat's boyhood friend.

'He's going to put up some shelves in the basement.'

'Can I talk to him a minute?'

'No,' said Mrs. Cugat, and hung up.

'A perfect day, too,' muttered Mr. Cugat wistfully from behind the funny papers.

Hatted and gloved and ready for church, she came out on the porch an hour later to find him still sitting there. 'You'll find the key to the cellar door in the back hall,' she informed him pointedly.

Mr. Cugat threw down his papers with a sigh, rose, stretched and pulled up his trousers. 'Okay,' he said, 'where are my overalls?'

'Overalls?'

'Yes —'

Mrs. Cugat said she'd never seen him in a pair of overalls in her life. He looked pained.

'I had them the summer I worked on the ranch,' he explained patiently.

'That was three years before we were married. They were probably given away ages ago.'

But Mr. Cugat thought not. Why would anybody give away a perfectly good pair of overalls? They must be somewhere around.

'The only place I can think of is in that trunkful of stuff that your Aunt Edith sent over,' she suggested. 'It's way up in the attic and I'm not a bit sure where the key is. Can't you just wear an old pair of flannels?'

This, it appeared, was not to be thought of. Mr. Cugat ascended to the attic. Dubiously, she left him there.

And found him, to her dismay, still there when she got back. 'Come up and look here a minute!' he shouted happily in answer to her call.

He hadn't found the overalls, but he'd found a lot of other things. Old class books, photographs of teams and glee clubs, a bundle of letters from a girl named Ada, and goodness knows what! Mrs. Cugat looked ruefully around the attic.

'Dinner!' trumpeted Anna, two flights below. Mr. Cugat's jaw dropped in astonishment.

The afternoon shadows lengthened, and he dozed in the porch swing. Mrs. Cugat bent over him with compassion. Poor darling, he was working so hard. His face looked drawn and very thin. She shook his shoulder, feeling like a brute. 'If you're going to get at those shelves —' she began.

Mr. Cugat blinked, glanced at his watch, and rose with alacrity. 'Jeepers, yes,' he said, 'how'd it get so late?' And without more ado, leapt down the steps and disappeared around the corner of the house. She followed him anxiously to see if there was anything she could do to help and found him already behind the garage, stalwartly shouldering lumber, a Louderback watching lynx-eyed.

'Where you going with them boards?' it was inquiring suspiciously.

Mr. Cugat grunted. 'Down cellar.'

'Why?'

'Building shelves.'

'*Building shelves!*' shrilled the mite and proceeded to go off into fits of typically derisive Louderback laughter. 'What you going to *keep* on the shelves?' it piped, when it could speak.

'Elephant eggs,' whispered Mr. Cugat and, swinging around to leer, accidentally caught the Louderback neatly with the end of the board and knocked it flat.

11

Screams of 'He hit me, Mamma!' rent the Sunday quiet as Mrs. Cugat hastened apprehensively across the street after them to explain. Mr. Cugat, callously, had continued on his way.

But when she got home, a bad half-hour later, she found him back in the porch swing. 'We haven't any saw!' he explained, surprised and indignant.

'Oh,' said Mrs. Cugat blankly.

He shook his head and sighed. 'You women! There's nothing in the tool drawer but an old hammer, a bent screwdriver and a funny-looking thing.'

'Well, up to now—' she began a little sharply, but he cut her short.

'Every household ought to have a good set of tools,' he declared, adding kindly, 'I'll buy you some in the morning.'

Mrs. Cugat sat down wearily. 'Did you leave all those boards in the laundry?' she asked.

'I never got them that far,' he grumbled. 'They were so long, I couldn't turn the corner and, as I say, I had no saw, so I had to leave them in the areaway. I'm afraid it makes it a little hard to get in and out —'

Somewhat to her surprise, he bought the tools the next day. A beautiful set of them, in a chest, and after dinner took each out and examined it enthusiastically. Mrs. Cugat kept a watchful eye on him, but, in handling something or other called an adze, he managed, as usual, to draw blood. Doctor Buell arrived and took a small stitch in him. Another Sunday came and went. That week the laundress kicked over a second bottle of wine and got a misery in her back — presumably from going through the areaway at a crouch.

Then Mr. Cugat was sent to Washington again! Really, it was getting to be the limit! Nice, of course, that out of the whole office he was always the one chosen to go, but he was worn out from being on the sleeper so much and trying to catch up with his regular work in between. She was getting sick and tired of being left alone, too. And all for nothing! She felt like speaking to Mr. Atterbury. As for Mr. Cugat, she felt like speaking to him and was going to. If he put those shelves off one more week, she'd call Allerton's, regardless. 'I'm going to call Allerton's, regardless, if you don't get those shelves built *this* week,' she said when, obviously still unremarked by Morgenthau, the seat of his trousers shiny, he came wearily home once again. 'The laundress is looking for another place and I don't blame her! The cellar's a shambles!'

Mr. Cugat admitted that this was so and on Sunday after lunch, meekly, and of his own accord, called Cory, cancelled his golf and prepared to get down to work. 'You didn't find my overalls?' he asked hopefully.

'No,' said Mrs. Cugat.

'Did you look?'

'No,' she said again flatly.

He picked up his new tools and descended to the cellar.

An hour passed, during which he could be seen toiling back and forth from the garage to the basement carrying more boards — four Louderbacks watching from a respectful distance — and then a reassuring pounding began. Better stay upstairs, she reasoned sensibly, so as not to distract him. Zitzawk, zit-zawk, went Mr. Cugat's new saw. Mrs. Cugat, inspired to industry, got out some darning. How nice, having him at home on a Sunday, busy around the house instead of off playing golf all day! Twenty busy minutes went by, and then the front door slammed. Hastening to the bannister, she peered over just in time to see Cory and an unreliable crony named Bill Stone making purposefully for the cellar stairs. Good Lord! She waited uncertainly, but, to her relief, the sawing began again almost immediately. Reassured, she went back and sat down. Maybe they'd just come over to

13

help. She had little confidence in either of them, but three heads should be better than one.

The darning was finished before it suddenly dawned on her that the sound of the hammer and the saw had been silent for some time. Quickly suspicious, she went to the cellar stairs and opened the door. A sweet intermingling of Mr. Cugat's mellow baritone, Cory's lilting tenor, and Mr. Stone's husky bass came up the stairs. *We're poor little lambs that have gone astray — Baa, baa, baa.* She hurried down.

The warblers were sitting comfortably on the floor with their backs against the wall and their legs outstretched. They were covered with sawdust and hung with shavings and their hair was curled with sweat. Between them was a sticky glass pitcher, half-full. Three empty wine bottles, an orange squeezer, a bag of lemons, and a plate of cookies were on the ironing-board. They greeted her with enthusiasm and pointed excitedly to the opposite wall. 'Look at the shelves!' they chorused proudly. 'All done!'

Mrs. Cugat looked.

The shelves, a palsied structure in four staggered sections, towered cautiously to the ceiling. 'Darling,' she exclaimed, 'so *many!*' The artisans beamed. 'What makes them lean forward like that?' she asked hesitantly.

Mr. Cugat considered them with care, head on one side, brow furrowed. Then he lifted the pitcher, drank, and got, rather painfully, to his feet. 'We don't quite know,' he said anxiously. 'Do you think it will make any difference?'

Mrs. Cugat touched the erection carefully and it swayed gently back and then forward again. 'It would be awful,' she said, 'if it tipped over.'

'I thought of taking this clothesline,' said Cory, rising, 'and tieing the whole thing to those pipes up there —' Mr. Stone took the pitcher absently from Mr. Cugat and started to lift it

14

to his lips, but, recollecting himself, politely passed it first to Mrs. Cugat.

'A little sheep dip?' he asked politely.

Mrs. Cugat sipped gingerly.

'Did you look at the shelves in the fruit room?' she ventured, after a little. 'It seems to me they're nailed to the wall in some way.'

'There's a different principle involved here, entirely,' said Mr. Cugat with dignity.

In the end, after another experimental pitcher-full, made this time — at Mr. Stone's suggestion — with just a dash of gin, it seemed sensible to adopt Cory's suggestion and lash the shelves, more or less firmly, to the hot-water pipes. Mrs. Cugat hoped she wouldn't be there when Anna got her first look at this arrangement. But she found suddenly, after one or two more critical sips, that the mundane concerns of tomorrow seemed far away and inconsequential. Lightheartedly, they repaired to the kitchen to make sandwiches.

Mr. Cugat's alarm clock rang stridently at half-past seven next morning and Mrs. Cugat turned her head with a groan. Mr. Cugat, bobbing up like an automaton, in the other bed, sank suddenly back on his pillow with a sharp exclamation. She blinked at him. His headache must be even worse than hers. That awful wine, of course. His eyes were wide and staring. 'I can't move,' he said. She sat up on the edge of her bed and tried to concentrate and he tried, again, to struggle upright and sank back. 'I think I've hurt myself.'

'Can I help you?' she asked dazedly, going over and putting an arm around his shoulders. She gave a little tug. Mr. Cugat yelped. 'George!' she exclaimed, really alarmed, 'what is it?'

'Well, I slipped off that ladder once yesterday,' he admitted sheepishly.

'I'd better call the doctor.'

Back from the phone, she hovered over him sympathetically with a hot-water bag. 'Doctor Buell is coming right over,' she said, 'and I called the office and told them you wouldn't be down. The office,' she added, with a little gleam, 'were frightfully upset. They said Mr. Atterbury was going to Washington again today and you were supposed to go with him. I told them this was one time he'd have to get along with somebody else.'

Mr. Cugat quivered beneath the covers. 'My God!' he groaned despairingly, 'He'll have to take Bemis and he'll make a fine mess of things! Give me the phone!' But at that moment, Doctor Buell arrived.

Mrs. Cugat retired to the hall to wait, anxious, but not greatly alarmed. Men were babies about such things. Besides, it would do Mr. Cugat no harm to have a day or two in bed, he was worn out. If Bemis made a fine mess of sitting around in waiting-rooms, so much the better, it would make Mr. Cugat's sitting around all the more appreciated. The doorbell rang and she went down to answer it, Anna being busy in the basement, dourly and without comment, transferring her jellies from the fruit room to their new home. She opened the door to confront no less person than Mr. Atterbury.

'What's all this I hear about George?' he rumbled, bustling in. 'It can't be anything serious. Let me see him! Is he up here?' He started for the stairs.

'The doctor's with him,' Mrs. Cugat protested, fluttering after him. But Mr. Atterbury kept right on going.

'George, my boy,' he bellowed, 'you in here?'

Mr. Cugat was lying on his stomach, face contorted. Doctor Buell was poking at the small of his back.

'By Gad, George, you've got to get up!' exclaimed the source of Mr. Cugat's income, breathlessly, from the foot of

16

the bed. 'We've got to be in Washington in the morning!'

'It's his sacro-iliac,' said Doctor Buell blandly — 'he couldn't get to Washington tomorrow if the President was expecting him.'

Mr. Atterbury waved his arms. 'That's just it, you fool!' he bellowed. 'The President *is* expecting him! Early's asked us to lunch!'

Mr. Cugat strove agonizingly. Doctor Buell probed hopefully. Mrs. Cugat wept. But it was no use — Mr. Cugat couldn't even turn over.

Mr. Atterbury, at length, threw up his hands. 'Well, I'll have to take Bemis, I suppose,' he growled, consulting his watch. 'He's a good man, though, Bemis — fine strong fella.'

Without another glance at poor Mr. Cugat, he clumped disgustedly out of the room and down the stairs unattended — Mrs. Cugat being too prostrate to move. The front door slammed awfully and the house shook. Then — far below them — came a muffled crash, a thin scream. Mr. Cugat's shelves had tipped over.

17

2

THOU SHALT NOT KILL

'Pull!' said Mrs. Cugat clearly, and a dark disk shot into the air in front of her and soared swiftly over her head. In one nicely co-ordinated action she raised her shotgun, pivoted smoothly and squeezed the trigger. The disk shattered and the imprisoned breath of some fifty onlookers escaped with a sigh — a sigh almost immediately overtaken by a surge of applause. She lowered the gun, broke its smoking breech, and smiled. Then her heart started to pound. She'd done it! The crowd closed in. 'Atta *girl*, Liz!' — 'Boy! What a performance!' — 'You were *wonderful*, darling!' — 'Can you beat it? And with a four-ten, too!' Her eyes sought Mr. Cugat's. He was beaming like a lamp. All he said, however, was, 'That was okay, Baby,' and ruffled her hair. What she'd done was to win the Willis P. Parmenter Trophy Open Skeet Shoot!

The Trophy's defender, a Mr. Pelley, pushed his way through the crowd and offered a small, dry hand. 'Let me be the first,' he said bleakly, and was again swallowed up. The crowd chattered with satisfaction. Mr. Pelley's name had been engraved on the Trophy's base for five years now, and he was beginning to think, perhaps justifiably, that he owned the thing — also that he and Sergeant York were in a class by themselves. Nobody had ever liked Mr. Pelley very well anyway, and to have him finally put on ice by little Mrs. Cugat was *wonderful*.

Mrs. Cugat was one of the few women who had ever entered 'the P.T. Open.' It was deemed an important event not to be slowed up by the merely mediocre. Mr. Cugat had been a little startled when she'd calmly announced that she had sent her name in, and had shaken his head ruefully and declared she hadn't a chance — but he only half-believed it. Mrs. Cugat, the last person in the world you would have thought it of, to look at her, since she was small, blond, and wholly feminine, had an eye like a secret bomb-site. 'I always just seem to know I'm going to hit it, so I usually do,' she explained it simply. She had learned to shoot at an early age at summer camp, but like anything too easily mastered, it hadn't interested her much and she'd only lately discovered skeet — for which she used a four-ten. Mr. Cugat had gently suggested that for the Parmenter Trophy — perhaps a twenty? But she wouldn't hear of it. 'A twenty makes so much *noise*,' she'd protested.

At the end of the first round she'd found herself, much to her own and everybody else's amazement, tied with Mr. Pelley with twenty-three out of twenty-five and the gallery with her to a man. On the second round they'd tied again — each with a perfect score. The judges had then requested that they continued shooting singles until one of them missed — a gruelling business — and Mr. Pelley, for the first time in the memory of man, began to look a little rattled. Mrs. Cugat, with no idea that she could really win, had gone on knocking them down. Mr. Pelley had cracked.

Willis P. Parmenter, a goateed and revered sportsman in plus-fours and a Norfolk jacket, came forward bearing the Trophy. 'My dear,' he began, 'I am honored!' Having never had a chance to present his trophy to anybody except Mr. Pelley, whom he simply detested, he let himself go on Mrs. Cugat — comparing her lyrically to Diana, the Huntress, and one or two other minor crack shots, and winding up with an impulsive invitation to a day's shooting with him at his duck club. It is probable that Mr. Pelley, on hearing this, suffered a severe pain in the neck. For as many times as he had captured Mr. Parmenter's Trophy, he had never yet received an invitation to shoot at his duck club — and he would have cut off his ears for one. As would many another man.

Mr. Parmenter's duck club was the Bay Beach. It was over a hundred years old, and the memberships, if you could get one, cost ten thousand dollars. Mr. Cugat belonged to it, having inherited his membership from a rich great-uncle who had left him nothing else, and every year, once a week, during the duck season, if he could get away, he spent a night there, but Mrs. Cugat had never even seen the place — as few women had. There was no rule banning women from its famous door, but as each member was allowed but one guest a year and as an invitation to shoot there was to be prized above rubies, few women ever made it — women, of course, having no business in a good club, anyway. Its traditions, customs, and myths were legion; the excellence of its cellar, the lavishness of its table, the picturesqueness of its employees, famed in song and story. One heard (*ad nauseam*, if one were a wife) quaint tales of old Olaf the punter, rapturous praise of Mrs. McIntosh the cook, and, above all, fatuous accounts of the local game warden Eric Swain, who, to hear them tell it, was evidently a double distillation of Paul Bunyan, Daniel Boone, Hiawatha, and Tarzan. Wives were instinctively curious about the Bay Beach, but it had, somehow, managed to remain — even in these days of women, rampant and untrammelled — sacrosanct, male and inviolable.

Mrs. Cugat, riding home from the skeet shoot, the Parmenter Trophy clasped to her breast, bounced on the car seat with pleasure. 'I can hardly wait for the duck season to open,' she sighed happily, 'so I can go down to Bay Beach.'

'Don't be silly,' said Mr. Cugat.

She turned to look at him. 'Silly! What do you mean? You heard Mr. Parmenter ask me, didn't you? I wouldn't miss it for the world!'

'Good Lord, honey!' he protested, 'I'd feel like a fool bringing you down there. Everybody'd think I was crazy. Old Parmenter didn't mean it. If he did, the old boy must be finally in his dotage.'

'Well, I like that!' She flushed indignantly. 'I don't see why I shouldn't go, if I'm invited — just as much as anybody else! Anybody'd think to hear you all talk that the place was sacred or something!'

'It's a man's club,' said Mr. Cugat simply. 'Men need a place where they can get off alone.'

'Oh — pooh,' she said lightly. 'Men just like to say that. It makes them feel rugged or something.'

Mr. Cugat looked patient.

Mr. Parmenter, however — possibly in his dotage — at any rate, quite evidently at an age which cared nothing about feeling rugged, called in due time and made good his invitation. Mrs. Cugat was jubilant. As Mr. Parmenter was the president of the Bay Beach, there wasn't much Mr. Cugat could say. He looked dubious, but gave in gracefully and went about ordering her a kind of sheep-lined jacket that he particularly liked and procuring a hunting license for her.

Mrs. Cugat made sensible and masculine preparations, packing a sober little bag with flannel pajamas and removing her nail polish. Now that she was actually going, she found herself rather awed.

They left by bus late in the afternoon on a raw November day that boded no good to ducks — Mrs. Cugat looking small and meek and about ten years old in her new sheepskin coat and gripping her gun case tensely as she eyed with respect the other passengers who, in the main, were ruddy gentlemen similarly clothed, armed, and plainly licensed.

'Will there be very many there this week-end, do you think?' she whispered a little nervously.

'Never can tell,' replied Mr. Cugat, carefully stowing her gun and unbuttoning her jacket as if she *were* ten years old, 'but I hope Swain's there. He's the game warden, you know,' and added, as usual, 'One of the most wonderful fellows you ever met —'

The bus followed the shore line and made frequent stops — Willow Point, Beaver Creek, Little Bay — most of the ruddy gentlemen getting off at a place called Higgin's Marsh. Not members of *our* club, thought Mrs. Cugat, and watched complacently from the bus window as they piled into a rattletrap old station-wagon and went bumping off up the road. She saw the scudding clouds and bleak swampland pass with growing excitement.

'Bay Beach next,' Mr. Cugat finally announced.

Bay Beach, at first glance, appeared to be nothing but a rusty mail box. Leaning against it, however, was an ancient individual holding onto the handle of a child's express wagon. Mr. Cugat greeted him with enthusiasm. 'Hello, Otto,' he said, tossing their bags into the wagon. 'How'd the summer treat you?'

Otto could not complain. He ducked his head at Mrs. Cugat in acknowledgment of Mr. Cugat's introduction and spat with the air of one who had now seen everything. Mr. Cugat muttered a sheepish aside, 'Mr. Parmenter, y'know —' to which Otto replied, 'Yeah — I heard,' and they all started briskly off up the road, the little express wagon rattling at their heels.

Mrs. Cugat found herself, in less than five minutes, dwelling with more respect on the Higgin's Marsh station-wagon. Mr. Cugat had insisted, sternly, on heavy boots, wool socks, a flannel shirt, a fleece-lined cap, and long underwear — evidently thistle-lined. She had meekly put them all on, but she ought to have known better. Men were used to twice as many clothes as women. She pushed the fleece back from her damp hair, reflecting ruefully on her wave, and hopefully unbuttoned her coat.

'Going too fast for you?' asked Mr. Cugat, politely slowing.

'Oh, no! I'm all right,' she assured him hastily. But she wasn't — her feet felt like a pair of inflamed flatirons. In another five minutes, sodden and panting, she had climbed into the express wagon. One would have thought, she mused, trundling along backwards, that the Bay Beach with all its money could afford something a little better than this, but hers not to reason why, certainly.

To her relief, there was nobody on hand to witness her ignominious arrival. They rounded a bend in the road and there it was — the famous Bay Beach Clubhouse — but save for a few twinkling lights the scene was empty and windswept. She had always pictured it, somehow, a low, rambling building of peeled logs and stone chimneys, set in a grove of pines and furnished with moose heads and Indian blankets. She had forgotten that, although this was always referred to as 'the new clubhouse,' it had been erected in the late eighties and, like everything else of that era, whether it was a duck club or an opera house, was invariably turreted gingerbread. It looked rather like a combination boathouse and bandstand, was painted a dark puce, and had, of all things, a bed of cannas before its door — with 'Bay Bridge' picked out in whitewashed stones in the grass. A row of willows wept behind it and behind them the marsh stretched away into the horizon.

Mrs. Cugat climbed out of the express wagon and limped up the front steps. An old black retriever, lying before the door, sprang to his feet and barked sharply. Then a vast rouged woman, with a jutting bust and pearl earrings, appeared around the corner of the porch. 'Down, Rex, you old sassbox, you!' she crooned, and explained to Mrs. Cugat lightly,

'That's Mr. Swain's dog, y'know. He's not used to women around.' She turned to greet Mr. Cugat more hospitably, however. 'I had to put you in number five, George,' she apologized, 'your own room having just the one bed, you know —'

'That's all right, Mac,' he said understandingly.

'Dinner won't be until eight o'clock tonight,' she added with a simper. 'Mr. Swain's coming.'

'I'm getting sick of this man Swain already,' muttered Mrs. Cugat, toiling up the tall stairway to number five. 'He'd better be good.'

Mr. Cugat, ahead of her, kicked open a door. 'Wait 'til you meet him,' he said. 'Women eat out of his hand — not that it's his fault,' he added loyally.

'I'll bet,' she murmured, but not very loud, being anxious to please, and sat down on the floor in the cold narrow room and began, relievedly, to unlace her boots.

'Hi, Cugat,' said a friendly voice in the doorway and a nice-looking young man in his long underwear — one hundred per cent wool, drop seat — sauntered in, gave Mrs. Cugat one incredulous look, glared at Mr. Cugat, and bolted out again.

Mr. Cugat went to the door, called, 'Sorry, Penrith,' and closed it gently.

'Maybe this was a mistake, after all,' she murmured apologetically. Mr. Cugat remained, rather obviously, silent.

Entering the big living-room for cocktails half an hour later, however, assurance was somewhat bolstered. Eight or nine men, seated around a stove, rose instantly, as though they had been only waiting, and Mr. Parmenter himself advanced to meet her. 'Ah,' he said, 'at last! Our little Diana!' Then, turning to the others, explained why they were thus honored. Admiration and respect shone from every eye — save, possibly, Mr. Penrith's, whose eyes were downcast, and Mr. Cugat stopped acting sheepish and grinned modestly. Two very nice

duck hunters from Pittsburgh pulled up a chair for her between their own and a colored man in a white coat brought her a martini. A toast was proposed and drunk. Mrs. Cugat looked around her curiously. The room was large and its furnishing heterogeneous, even including a pair of bead portières, but it had an air. Faded group photographs of early hirsute members, framed letters, Audubon prints, and mounted fish covered the walls, but new magazines, big chromium ashtrays, and innumerable match packs advertising a dog food strewed its tables. The stove was black and ancient — the linoleum, bright and new. The mantel bore a triangular-faced electric clock of green plastic and an old pair of duelling pistols. There was a china umbrella stand full of gilded cattails in one corner and an upright piano. That no interior decorator had ever set foot here — and survived — was evident, but there was something about it, at that, that any decorator would barter his soul to achieve. The new linoleum came up for discussion and was highly approved. Its pattern, an occasional yellow blob on a field of black and gray lozenges, it was agreed was just the thing! It was not going to show the dirt the way that old red carpet had. Mrs. McIntosh herself had suggested linoleum and picked it out. No surprise to Mrs. Cugat.

Another round of cocktails came in, followed by Mrs. McIntosh herself, bearing a bowl of popcorn. 'This'll keep you going,' she said with a motherly beam, "til Mr. Swain gets here,' and they thanked her extravagantly. It was store popcorn and quite stale, Mrs. Cugat discovered, but nobody seemed to know the difference. Mrs. Cugat's health was drunk again and the two duck hunters from Pittsburgh waxed gallant and decided to flip a coin to see which would play gin rummy with her after dinner. Mr. Parmenter twinkled at her fondly, Mr. Cugat beamed, Mr. Penrith stopped blushing. Wagers were laid on how long it would take her to get her limit on the following day and the odds were flattering. She began to feel gay, witty, and rather special. Then the front door slammed and a booming, hearty laugh filled the house. Swain, at last. Several men took their glasses and went out to greet him. He could be heard announcing in a pleasantly deep voice that he was hungry enough to eat mule meat, which was followed by the sound of a smart spank, a tittering protest from Mrs. McIntosh, and general laughter. There came a headlong series of chimes. 'Dinner!' exclaimed everybody joyfully.

'May I?' inquired Mr. Parmenter, offering his arm, and Mrs. Cugat gulped her martini.

Mr. Swain, as they entered the dining-room, was standing at the sideboard, surrounded by an admiring group and making himself a highball. Mrs. Cugat took one look at him and wished desperately for her lipstick. Mr. Swain looked like Cary Grant. Instead of the plaid mackinaw and fur cap with a tail, in which her always too fanciful imagination had dressed him, he was wearing a grey flannel suit, a blue polka-dotted tie, and a seal ring with a crest on it.

Mr. Parmenter hastened forward with elaborate introductions and, spurred by martinis, launched off into a fulsome account of Mrs. Cugat's prowess. Mr. Swain looked very polite but acutely bored. Feeling like a fool, she raised her eyebrows coolly — there being nothing much else to do. Why, the conceited donkey! Who did he think he was, anyway? If he was so wonderful, why wasn't he in the Army? She would ignore him.

But this proved to be embarrassingly easy. Mr. Swain waited until she had been gallantly seated by little Mr. Penrith at Mr. Parmenter's right and then pointedly went and sat at the farthest end of the long table with the two Pittsburgh hunters following like adoring puppies. The others sorted themselves out, the youngest and most agile winning in a scramble for seats nearest the warden, and Mrs. Cugat found herself between Mr. Parmenter and his equally ancient brother-in-law and across from Mr. Cugat and a saturnine little man who appeared to be stone deaf. Scornfully, she kept her eyes from travelling to the other end any oftener than was necessary, but it was not easy.

The other end were sent, almost immediately, into stitches. They sobbed with mirth and rolled in their chairs. Mrs. Cugat had to admit, from an occasional scrap that floated her way, that Mr. Swain was something of a wit — but didn't he know it! Black eyes wickedly alight, his grin sardonic, he dominated the entire conversation. 'Regular cut-up, aren't you?' she muttered bad-temperedly as his voice dropped discreetly to finish the current side-splitter. Mr. Cugat soberly discussed pintails with Mr. Parmenter. She turned again to the brother-in-law and dutifully caught up on his rambling tale of a 1908 snowstorm. 'Just you wait until after dinner, my fine friend!' she vowed under her breath. 'I'll make you take some notice of me — see if I don't!' and aloud politely murmured, anent the snowstorm, 'It hardly seems possible!'

But at the end of the meal, when they rose to go into the other room, Mr. Swain merely stood for a moment courteously and then sat down again, in obvious relief, and ordered another cup of coffee. Several, including the two Pittsburgh hunters (who had apparently forgotten all about gin rummy), drew up chairs to remain with him. The dining-room door closed, but as their muffled laughter came through to those settling around the stove, one after another of them got up and sauntered back. Mrs. Cugat found herself, finally, alone with Mr. Parmenter, Mr. Cugat having gone out to the kennels to see about his dog. Conversation died and Mr. Parmenter dozed shamelessly. Then she heard a voice from the dining-room suggest moving away from the table and a drawling rejoinder by the game warden to the effect that he was in no mood for lady huntresses named 'Dinah' and what the hell was the place coming to? Mrs. Cugat got quietly to her feet and tiptoed out of the room, her cheeks hot. Crude, ill-mannered boor! One of those overcharged males who like to fancy themselves 'just a man's man'! Odious type. She paused irresolutely at the foot of the stairs, hating to go to bed yet — since it was only a little after nine o'clock. A half-open door, along the hall, revealed a pleasantly lighted room with red curtains and she peered timidly in. The gun room. Well, this would give her something to do until Mr. Cugat came back. She could go in and quietly look around without, she hoped, discommoding the great Swain too much.

The walls were lined with racks of shotguns. There was a glass cabinet of old service revolvers and a row of ancient rifles. Above the racks ran a crowded frieze of stuffed birds — very old stuffed birds, judging by the dust. In their midst, however, in a handsome glass case, was another — a disagreeable-looking, hump-backed creature posed uncomfortably on one leg amid some imitation bulrushes. Mrs. Cugat went over to read the brass plate at the base of its case. *Sacred Ibis* (*Threskiornis aethiopica*), *killed by Eric Van R. Swain, April 19, 1938, Blue Nile, Egypt*, it said. The corners of Mrs. Cugat's mouth turned down and she turned her attention to the guns — running her fingers lightly along the row of polished stocks. There was no dust here. The dark woods gleamed like satin and the barrels were sleek with grooming. Timidly, she lifted a graceful little rifle from its place and balanced it appreciatively. Smiling at the way it handled, she pulled up on the Sacred Ibis. She must try a rifle again, some day. She went on to another rack.

This one stood a little apart, and Mrs. Cugat bent to examine its contents with an exclamation of pleasure. Here was evidently the cream of the collection — some real beauties! An English Holland and Holland — what looked like a Parker A.H.E. Gently, she lifted out a little, long-barrelled

28

over-and-under to look at the chasing. It was a peculiarly made gun — like none she'd ever seen. She broke the breech curiously, wondering what size the bore was — it looked too small for a twenty. On a table beside her were several opened boxes of shells and she selected one and experimentally slipped it in. Well, she was wrong — it was a twenty — full choke evidently. Interested, she pulled up on the Ibis again. There was a quick growl of warning, a snarl — and she staggered forward under the impact of a leaping curly body. A blast like a cannon's split the air.

Opening her eyes, she found herself looking into the grave face of Mr. Swain. Rex, the black retriever, pompously guarded the gun rack; across the room lay the Sacred Ibis without any head. The two Pittsburgh hunters, from the hall, hurried over to it with cries of dismay. Mr. Swain cleared his throat. 'We-ll,' he drawled, 'getting in a little practice?'

Mrs. Cugat sputtered. 'That dog —' she began.

'I'm sorry,' he said coldly. 'But he resents strangers handling my guns,' and stooping, picked up the little shotgun from the débris on the floor and carefully ejected the empty cartridge. There was a deep, new scratch on the stock where it had hit against something sharp in falling. He ran his finger along it gently and then turned, without a word, and left the room.

A shocked cortège bearing the Sacred Ibis moved toward the wastebasket. '*You're* all right, I hope,' one of them said belatedly as she moved to let them pass.

She awoke, however, in the dark early morning, mortification assuaged and shivering with excitement. Mr. Cugat was already dressed. 'Get your clothes on,' he ordered, 'and meet me down in the dining-room. There'll be coffee.' She hurried out of bed and into her things.

The dining-room was brightly lighted and empty, save for Mr. Cugat, but a sleepy colored boy brought a steaming cup and a plate of toast. 'Drink up,' Mr. Cugat urged. 'We're late — most of the others have gone.'

She obediently managed one or two swallows. 'I don't believe I care for much,' she apologized, after a minute or two. 'I can never seem to eat when I'm excited, you know, it makes me feel like throwing up —'

'For the love of Pete,' he exclaimed anxiously, 'try not to.'

But out in the sharp, black morning queasiness passed and she followed him and his obedient little retriever, Mellow, eagerly along the narrow planks leading across the marsh.

'Thanks to you, Diana, we drew the walk-out blind,' said Mr. Cugat with satisfaction, 'and it's a honey. You can get your limit out here in half an hour with a sling-shot. Mr. Parmenter,' he went on, 'usually has his name on it, but I guess, for you, he'd give up anything.' She began to feel more lighthearted.

The walk-out blind was a comfortable little shelter made of cornstalks with a wooden floor and a bench. It had a roof that popped open like a jack-in-the-box. Sitting inside, close to Mr. Cugat, their thermos, sandwiches, and other belongings cosily arranged, she felt that same delicious snugness she'd felt as a child when she'd found a new playhouse in some secret place. She cuddled impulsively closer to him and rubbed her cheek against his sleeve.

'Now, now,' he said impassively, 'no necking.'

The sun came up and the empty sky grew bright. From time to time somebody with a duck call quacked forlornly near at hand. Half an hour passed and she shifted stiffly and smothered a yawn, regarding Mr. Cugat's quiet profile tenderly. He was really very good-looking, particularly in these outdoor clothes. He sat motionless, his gun over his arm, occasionally flicking the ash from his cigarette.

30

'What are you thinking about?' she asked gently.

'I was thinking that we ought to get around to making your will,' he said cheerfully. 'We keep putting it off. You'd better come down to the office some day *next* week and we'll talk it over with Benson.'

She subsided and the usual depressing train of thought that this particular subject set in motion — morbid speculation on Mr. Cugat's probable way of life after she was gone — got under way.

'What does the club pay that Mrs. McIntosh?' she asked suddenly, arriving at an unexpected destination.

Surprised, Mr. Cugat named a figure.

She exclaimed indignantly. 'For what that woman does? That's perfectly ridiculous!'

'It's a lot,' admitted Mr. Cugat, 'but she's worth it. We'll never find another like her!' Mrs. Cugat laughed shortly. 'Look at that dinner last night,' he went on dotingly, 'where else could you get a meal like that?'

'There wasn't a *single* green vegetable!'

'I should hope not!' he exclaimed fervently.

'And canned soup and drugstore ice cream! When she could just as well have made them herself. Plain lazy — that's what she is — if you want the truth!'

'You wanted to come,' said Mr. Cugat mildly; 'nobody asked you to like it.'

Mrs. Cugat, stung, subsided again somewhat guiltily and tried to slip her icy toes, unnoticed, under Mellow's belly. Mellow looked reproachful and got up and went outside to squat, shivering.

'Whatsa matter, girl?' crooned Mr. Cugat in concern.

'Have you ever done anything about asking Mr. Atterbury to raise your salary?' asked Mrs. Cugat brightly, by way of changing the subject.

'No,' he said shortly.

'I don't see why not!' she countered with new energy. 'You certainly deserve it — all this extra Washington work and everything!' And added, in a familiar tone, 'What's the matter — are you afraid of him or something?'

'Do we have to go into all that again — *here?*' he protested. 'This is supposed to come under the head of fun, you know. Good Lord! Why can't a woman just sit still once in a while and enjoy herself!'

'You started it,' she sniffed — 'bringing up that old will again. I suppose that comes under the head of fun! Fun for you, maybe — sitting there planning what you're going to do when I'm dead and out of the way! Why don't you just move out here with your wonderful Mrs. McIntosh and end up with a good case of beri-beri?'

Mr. Cugat did not bother to answer this and she retired, ashamed. Why was it that husbands and wives so often got off onto the wrong things at the wrong time! If she were sitting out here with anybody else, she would be exerting every effort to be charming, interested and entertaining, but here she was, all cosy in a duck blind with Mr. Cugat whom she adored, and for some reason their every pet bone of contention had perversely come to light. There were some aspects of married life that were inexplicable and depressing. She moved her feet gently and found them completely numb. The sun had subsided and a raw wind sprung up. 'This ought to bring them in!' Mr. Cugat observed happily. Maybe if she loosened her bootlaces, she thought, and resting her gun in a corner, bent over to tug at the laces with stiff fingers. Something cold, hard, and crawling lit on her bare neck and scampered for cover down her back. 'E-e-e-e-ek!' she squealed, knocking her gun over and trampling on Mellow's tail. Mellow yipped in agony and disappeared.

'What *is* it?' cried Mr. Cugat.

'Oh — I don't *know!* Something perfectly huge and awful is down my back!'

'Spider, maybe,' he suggested helpfully.

She tore at the buttons of her collar. 'Oh, darling!' she chattered, finally loosening it, 'reach down quick and see! It's probably a black widow — I was just reading about them in the *Reader's Digest* —' Mr. Cugat, unflurried, stood his gun in a corner, took off his glove and investigated. She could feel whatever it was stirring warily in any one of six different places.

A sudden din of squawking rose from their neighbor with the duck call. 'Here they come,' said Mr. Cugat grimly, his hand imprisoned down her back. Six pairs of rhythmically flapping wings travelled low over their heads and sank out of sight in the pond behind them. But Mrs. Cugat had forgotten all about ducks.

'Have you found it?' she quavered.

Mr. Cugat removed his hand and arm and looked down.

'I don't see a goddamned thing,' he muttered.

She shook herself tentatively and could feel nothing.

'It's gone,' she said weakly. 'Oh dear! Do you suppose it was a spider?'

'No,' said Mr. Cugat shortly. 'Spiders hibernate in weather like this. Probably some little piece of cornstalk or something.' She buttoned her shirt doubtfully. 'That was a beautiful bunch of blacks that came in just now,' he sighed wistfully, but Mrs. Cugat was still absorbed in her spider.

'They say you can tell a black widow because it has red spots on its stomach,' she vouchsafed, 'and five minutes after you've been bitten, you're unconscious.'

'Evidently, you've been spared,' observed Mr. Cugat.

She huddled into her collar and tried to keep her teeth from chattering. Her feet had passed the numb stage and progressed to aching. How could she, in the same clothes, be so hot yesterday and so cold today? Look at Mr. Cugat! Warm and comfortable — his exploring fingers had been like toast — and yesterday, when she'd been dripping with perspiration, he'd been *cool* and comfortable. Men were wonderful!

'Here come some more!' he exclaimed suddenly in an eager whisper. 'Got your gun? You take the first shot.'

Six black specks on the horizon took form and life. The man with the duck call quacked frenziedly and four swiftly winging shapes swooped down. Mrs. Cugat lifted her gun. Then she wavered and slowly lowered it; Mr. Cugat's gun cracked a split second later, and one of the sailing shapes hurtled down. Mellow splashed into the water. 'What happened to you?' he queried, turning, eyes alight.

'Oh, George,' she said, chagrined, 'I don't know! Just as I was on one, he sort of leaned out and looked down over his wing like an aviator. I simply *couldn't!* It was the cutest thing you ever saw! And now the poor thing's dead —' she mourned, as a dripping Mellow came triumphantly back with a big mallard in her mouth.

'But that was the main idea in coming out here, wasn't it?' asked Mr. Cugat curiously. 'To shoot ducks, I mean —'

'I know,' she said, miserably. 'I'm a perfect idiot, but I didn't have any idea I'd feel this way.' She took Mellow's limp burden from her and gently stroked the shimmering green feathers. 'I never was the sporting type, I guess. It's just an accident that I can shoot — I hate to kill anything and always have.' Two tears splashed down unnoticed.

'Wait 'til you've missed one or two,' Mr. Cugat said, comfortingly, 'you'll get over that! It's not easy.'

'I don't believe I ever will,' she sighed, sitting down despondently, still holding the dead duck. Mr. Cugat produced a handkerchief and handed it to her kindly. 'Look, darling,' she said, after a minute or two, 'you stay here and enjoy yourself and I'll walk in. For some reason, I seem to be blue with

34

cold and I'm nothing but a trouble to you. My hands ache so, I doubt if I could hit anything even if I wanted to.'

He protested vigorously, but she insisted and, breaking her gun, dropped a kiss on his cheek, ducked stiffly out the little door and started off across the marsh toward the clubhouse. She was a fine one, she was! Mr. Cugat had been perfectly right about her coming down here — she'd been a perfect nuisance and made him look like a softie in front of his friends. But right now she was too cold to care. She couldn't care about anything, even Mr. Cugat, until she got warmer. Maybe that colored boy could make her a hot toddy or something. She looked up out of her collar to see how far off realization of this possibility was and encountered a strolling figure, coming toward her. Swain! Of all people! And there was no escaping him either — there was only one narrow walk and they were both on it. He was walking slowly with his head down, the black retriever at his heels. He was dressed for the part this time — laced boots, breeches, hunting cap, and parka with a fur-lined hood. A cigarette hung nonchalantly from the corner of his mouth. She hurriedly tucked up a straggling lock and wiped her tears. Her cheeks, so lately cold, flushed hot with chagrin. She could just imagine the cutting humor with which he would, forever after, embellish the tale of the Sacred Ibis and the amusement in his black eyes when he heard that she'd proved such a sissy. She lifted her head defiantly. Well, let him have his fun! She'd probably never see him again, anyway. There was a loud whirring in front of her and something soared suddenly into the air. She raised her gun, fired, and it came plummeting down. Wholly startled, she looked toward Swain. He'd stopped dead in his tracks and was looking at her. A flood of pleasant exultation welled up and she started to tremble. 'There! fancy-pants,' she muttered, 'I'm not such a dud after all, am I?' She smiled and waved casually. Mr. Swain did not re-

35

turn the salute, but turned and said something to his dog who bounded off. There was a splashing and crashing behind her and Mr. Cugat emerged, white-faced, from the blind.

'Are you all right?' he shouted, and then, as he drew closer, panted, 'Good God! What was that shot? I thought you'd probably fallen and blown your head off!'

'Not at all,' she explained, with dignity as the warden strolled up, 'I was just walking along and a duck went up in front of me, so I shot it.' Mr. Swain's dog came out through the reeds and Mr. Cugat stopped suddenly, dead in his tracks. 'What a funny-looking duck!' exclaimed Mrs. Cugat.

Mr. Swain stooped and took the bird gently from the dog's mouth. 'Isn't it?' he said. Then he gave Mr. Cugat a long and sympathetic look.

Mr. Cugat sighed. 'That's a hen pheasant, honey,' he said resignedly. 'The fine is fifty dollars.'

3

THOU SHALT NOT STEAL THY
NEIGHBOR'S THUNDER

W HEW!' sighed Mr. Cugat, setting down his suitcase in the
front hall and tossing his overcoat over the newel post, 'it's
good to be home!' He kissed Mrs. Cugat with satisfaction.
'Anything happen while I was away?'

'Nothing much,' Mrs. Cugat said, tenderly gathering up the
overcoat and carrying it off to the hall closet. She hurried
back, bright-eyed and beaming. 'Did you have a nice trip?'

Mr. Cugat made weary tracks for the lavatory. 'Lousy,' he
said. 'Ask Anna if I have time for a drink before dinner.'

'Dinner can wait,' she said, comfortingly. 'I'll fix you a
highball,' and sped, humming, to the pantry.

Mr. Cugat had been away for ten days. In Washington.
Things, of course, *had* happened since he'd been gone about
which she could hardly wait to tell him, but it was better, she'd
found, to give him a moment or two before she started in.
That is, if she wanted full and sympathetic attention. Mr.
Cugat was apt to be a little abstracted right after a trip to
Washington.

He recovered rather more quickly than usual after this one,
however, and stretched back comfortably in his chair and
twinkled at her fondly and sipped his highball. She'd made
it rather strong. 'Well, spill it,' he said indulgently, 'before
you burst.' So she told him first about the trouble with the

37

hot-water heater and the plumber's verdict that the pipes were 'gone,' and then about Charlie calling up from the bank to say that she was overdrawn again (only she wasn't — she could prove it), and then about the laundress being impudent and the neighbors' threats to poison Lillian and the Carradines' picnic for Elsa Maxwell and the two Chinese generals visiting the Blakes. Then she said, a little too casually, 'Oh, yes, and such a *pathetic* postcard came from your cousin Adela — I just wrote and told her to come and stay with us for a while —'

'You did *what?*' said Mr. Cugat. Mrs. Cugat plunged into culpable explanation. 'Cousin Adela!' he exclaimed, not even listening. 'My God!'

Anna, with a welcoming grin, announced dinner.

'I know you never cared much about the poor little thing,' Mrs. Cugat apologized, following him out to the dining-room, 'but she sounded so sad. We mustn't be narrow and selfish any more, you know. Think how you'd feel if you were fighting in India like what's-his-name and *I* was alone in a strange country with just our two babies.'

'Is what's-his-name out in India?' said Mr. Cugat, with a flicker of interest.

'Yes,' said Mrs. Cugat eagerly; 'way over there probably not knowing for months at a time where she is or what she's doing —'

'What a break for him!' he said, unfeelingly.

'George!' she protested, 'I don't think that's a bit funny in times like these. You might, at least, try to remember those poor babies!'

'I'm trying not to,' said Mr. Cugat. 'A couple of terrible-acting, buck-toothed brats. I never thought old what's-his-name liked them very well himself.'

'It's perfectly disgraceful of you to talk like that!' she exclaimed indignantly. 'What's the matter with you, anyway?

Would you like to have it said, you turned your own relatives out in the cold?'

'Where are these shivering waifs?' he inquired tartly.

'Newport — just now.'

Mr. Cugat looked eloquent. 'Well, it's your funeral,' he said, attacking his ham and eggs. 'Don't expect any help from me.'

'You make me sick!' she declared. 'A lot of people have been *glad* to take perfect strangers into their homes. Look at Evie and Howie!'

'Ah,' said Mr. Cugat, 'now I see.'

'What?' she queried crossly.

'Why all this sudden hospitality.'

'I don't know what you're talking about!' she protested.

'Why, all you gals have been burned up, and you know it, ever since Evie wangled little Lord Adenoid for the duration. But if you think those tots of Adela's will bear showing off, you're in for an awful disappointment.'

This was, actually, rather unfair of Mr. Cugat. It is true that Mrs. Sturm, dear but ever unsettling friend of Mrs. Cugat, *had* somehow wangled the Honorable Jeremy Spenser and his Nannie for the duration and was enjoying him to the hilt. She had even had her picture in *Vogue* — kneeling beside him on the grass, cheek pressed to his, while her own two infants stared fascinated from the rear — and had, really, according to the bridge club, not been fit to live with since. Not that there wasn't one of the bridge club who wouldn't have given a right arm to be harboring the Honorable Jeremy. He was perfectly adorable. He made everyone feel like a peasant when he was brought in to say good night at dinner parties. Those manners and that accent! And he was good in school and liked to eat. As for the Nannie who came with him! A Treasure! Already licking Evie's two mewling little girls into shape. Trust Evie to fall on her feet.

But Mrs. Cugat, to give her credit, really hadn't asked Mr. Cugat's cousin Adela and her babies to visit *entirely* for the sake of keeping up with the Sturms. Mrs. Cugat was a creature of intense and whole-hearted enthusiasms and her imagination impetuously flamed in response to any cause afoot. It required continual damping down. The picture immediately conjured up by Cousin Adela's postcard from Newport of a frail, grief-ridden young mother, chin-up to a strange world for the sake of her little ones while what's-his-name battled in India, had simply kindled unquenchable fires. Unquenchable, that is to say, with no Mr. Cugat on hand to quench them. She had impulsively written gathering Cousin Adela to her breast and Cousin Adela had written right back that they would arrive Monday-week. That it wouldn't hurt Evie Sturm a bit to have a little of her interminable thunder stolen was, however, undeniable. But nobody's motives were ever entirely unmixed, reasoned Mrs. Cugat, anxiously examining her own in the light of Mr. Cugat's cynical implications. She sincerely longed to comfort poor little Adela and her babies and make them feel less homeless. The English had been wonderfully brave; one wanted to do anything one could to help. Of course, Adela was only English by marriage, had a flock of relatives, and so was not exactly out in the street, but the idea was the same. Mrs. Cugat could hardly wait until she got here. Mr. Cugat would get used to the idea in a day or two — it was just that he'd been to Washington and was a little cross.

But Mr. Cugat's enthusiasm during the next few days remained dormant. He looked glum whenever Cousin Adela was mentioned and perversely side-stepped any discussion of plans, finally announcing, with obvious relief, that on December first, Mr. Atterbury was sending him back to Washington for another week. Mrs. Cugat, who ordinarily would have been disconsolate at this news, found herself rather relieved. This would give her a chance to get everybody settled down before he came back. And when he came back, he'd be surprised to find how smoothly things ran. She had everything beautifully planned to the last detail. Adela would have the big guest-room — its taffeta spreads and little lace chaise-longue pillows had been sent to the cleaners and a new thermos ordered. She was planning to have fresh flowers always on the dressing-table and Adela's breakfast sent up every morning on the new glass tray. She had bought a little white fur rug for in front of the fireplace and a big jar of lavender bath salts and a sponge. In the little guest-room, on the other side of the connecting bath, the babies could sleep — conveniently near. Until now, Mrs. Cugat had never done very much about the little guest-room and usually kept the door shut — it being furnished with an old ivory-painted bedroom set she'd had as a child and inadequately carpeted by a small rag rug — Anna kept the vacuum cleaner in there and salvaged wrapping paper — but all this was to be changed. Blue organdie curtains with Donald Duck on them were being run up by Miss Terry and china lamps supported by Donald only waited to be unwrapped. Her mother being away, the blue velvet rug, borrowed from her morning room, already made a different place of it. In the event of Adela's babies having a Nannie like the Honorable Jeremy — well, Anna would simply have to move over. But Anna's room was light and airy and the bed a double one — she probably wouldn't mind. She was always having that sister spend the night, wasn't she? (Mrs. Cugat had decided to wait, however, until the Nannie materialized before broaching the subject. Anna was something of a brooder, but had never failed in a pinch.) When Adela'd been here a day or two, she planned to give a small, carefully picked luncheon for her at the club. And then, when her mother got home from New York, she'd get her to have a big tea. 'To meet George's little cousin from London'

— 'perfectly pathetic, my dear, but so attractive' — 'yes, he's in India, but she's very brave —' Meanwhile, Cory would be over the first thing and probably fall in love with Adela — he could usually be counted on for this — which would be pleasant and distracting for her and very convenient because then he'd come every night and they could always have a bridge game or perhaps go out dancing once in a while. Mr. Cugat would have to go out dancing if they all worked on him. And it would be just what he needed — take his mind off Washington. Thus, she laid careful, innocent plans, facing Monday-week without presentiment.

Monday-week, however, came and went without advent; Tuesday likewise. Mrs. Cugat waited upon the telephone nervously and made four meals off a lobster mousse that had been too precipitously prepared. On Wednesday morning, however, without warning, a pure white station-wagon, driven by a colored man in a béret, appeared at the door and began to unload. Not passengers — baggage, of a peculiarly conglomerate appearance unmistakably English. Innumerable strapped and bulging bags, umbrellas, blanket rolls, tennis racquets, and parcels tied with string piled up in the hall; a sun lamp, a pneumatic mattress, a foot-bath, a dog-basket, an electric hair-dryer, what looked to be full equipment for colonic irrigation and an inexplicable roll of linoleum were stacked on the porch. The folks might arrive by afternoon the colored man said with no conviction: meanwhile would they just show him to his rooms, he'd like some rest. Mrs. Cugat had to do some fast thinking. However (with the help of a man who was raking leaves next door), the glider from the front porch, a table from the laundry, one of the dining-room chairs, and a rag rug were boosted to the loft of the garage and hastily arranged. The window in the loft of the garage having never been opened, the mean temperature there was about one hundred degrees Fahrenheit, and it was

full of dead flies, but the colored man, whose name was
Leonard, was quite nice about it and stoically retired. Mrs.
Cugat, subduing anxiety, left him on tiptoe and went back
to the porch to wait.

But by seven-thirty that night, the folks had yet to appear,
and, picking her way for the hundredth time through the
clutter in the hall, she went wearily to tell Anna not to go on
with dinner — just to fix her a little something on a tray.
Anna she found ominously quiet and frying potatoes: at the
kitchen table, napkin in his collar, Leonard, waiting politely.

At ten minutes after eleven, however, the telephone rang.
Mrs. Cugat, tumbling out of a bed she had just got into,
answered it dazedly. Mrs. Saint John, said an impeccable
male voice, pronouncing it 'Sinjin,' would arrive in about
half an hour and asked if there might be a little Bovril prepared, as she was very tired. Mrs. Cugat scrambled into her
clothes and dashed to the third floor. Anna, more ominously
silent than ever and with her hair in a braid, descended. Mrs.
Cugat flew around and lit the lamps again and brought up
vases of flowers just put away in the basement. Should she,
she wondered, rouse Leonard? Anna, however, here looked
up from wrenching the top off a can of tomato soup and
vouchsafed the information that Leonard had borrowed a
dollar from her and gone to town.

Mrs. Cugat's first sight of Cousin Adela was, of course, a
shock. There was the trouble with Mrs. Cugat. She had
known exactly what Adela would look like, how she would
act, what she would say. She had made up long and delightful conversations between herself and Adela and she had
grown, during them, very fond of her. That the Adela who
emerged from a Rolls town car at midnight was not Mrs.
Cugat's Adela was hardly surprising, but really, she was very
unforeseen. This Adela was middle-aged, roly-poly, and fret-
ful; with faded blond hair, a great many beads, and a coat

trimmed with monkey fur. She came up the walk, leaning heavily on the arm of a languid young woman, who was black as ebony, and sank panting to the settee in the front hall. 'My heart, y'know,' she gasped, smiling bravely up at Mrs. Cugat. 'Just give me a moment — a little brandy, perhaps —' Mrs. Cugat flew for Mr. Cugat's Napoleon.

'Aren't the babies with you?' she ventured anxiously as the patient seemed to revive.

'Aren't the babies with us, Myrtle?' inquired Cousin Adela interestedly.

'They was, but they stopped for a hot-dog,' said Myrtle. 'We want all this stuff upstairs, don't we?' She looked reproachfully at Mrs. Cugat.

'Yes, child, yes,' said Cousin Adela, passing a weary hand across her eyes. 'Have it seen to.'

'Supper,' said Anna, sticking her head in the door.

Mrs. Cugat took a deep breath. 'Is your chauffeur still outside?' she asked hopefully.

'If you mean Caldwell,' said Cousin Adela, 'I'm afraid not. He's Poppy Farnese's man. She sent me on in her car, dear thing. I can never go by rail, y'know. Air-conditioning.'

Mrs. Cugat desperately picked up a hatbox, an ancient golf cape, and a portable victrola and started for the stairs, but at that moment the babies sauntered in. They were tall, blond, divinely fair, and about eighteen. Each carried a Pekinese. 'We were utterly famished,' they explained in lovely voices, 'so we stopped in at a place for a sausage roll. Will someone see to our car?' There was a squeal of brakes, a flash of headlights, and a spray of gravel on the porch, and they turned and sauntered out again.

Mrs. Cugat flew after them. 'I say, your fence is down,' they called back at her.

'Who *is* it? What's happened?' she gasped, hurrying down the steps.

44

'Just old Leonard,' they laughed, pointing to the station-wagon in the middle of the front lawn, 'potted again.'

Four days later, Mrs. Cugat awoke to stare morosely at Donald Duck, holding up the lamp beside her bed. A small lake spread from under the bathroom door and lapped at the edge of her mother's blue velvet rug, but she regarded it without surprise. One of the babies had probably taken a shower in the night. One of the babies was always taking a shower, but neither baby ever thought to hang the curtain *in*side the tub. Sometimes the babies' showers lasted for hours at a time and one of these days the steam-sodden ceiling was going to come down on one of their beautiful heads. Which would be all right, too. Today was the day Mr. Cugat got home. Thank Heaven! How he would get her out of this mess, she couldn't imagine. But Mr. Cugat would do something. He wouldn't put up with this situation five minutes. Her eyes fell on Donald Duck cavorting across the curtains. Wait 'til Mr. Cugat found himself sleeping with Donald in the little guest-room! And he would find himself sleeping there because Cousin Adela had had to have their room. It was the only room with a dressing-room and Cousin Adela always had to have a room with a dressing-room so that Myrtle would be within call. Her heart y'know. You could stick pins in Myrtle and she wouldn't wake up, but Cousin Adela felt more comfortable when she was near — and anyway, in this case, one could hardly have demanded that Anna move over.

All idea of putting these Amazon babies, with their Pekineses, victrolas, and hair-dryers, in with Donald had had to be given up right at the start, of course. There simply wasn't room enough for them. They had been ensconced in the big guest-room and seemed fairly comfortable there, cosily cooking cocoa on a Sterno and eternally changing each other's nail polish while the Pekineses rooted happily among the lace pillows and jealously attacked the new fur rug.

Mrs. Cugat heard Anna come creakily down the back stairs. Anna, as far as anybody knew, had not spoken since Wednesday. Mrs. Cugat found it necessary to be often in the kitchen, but she carried on any conversation there with herself. 'Anna, Mrs. Saint John never eats starches, it seems. Could you just open a can of crabmeat or something quickly. Oh, good! Just bake it with a little cheese, I guess. My goodness — all those fried potatoes for breakfast! Well! Doesn't a man in the kitchen make a difference, though! It certainly does. Do you think we might try a soufflé tonight? No — well, I guess perhaps not —'

Anna rattled the milk bottles loudly and in her room down the hall Cousin Adela whimpered. Cousin Adela never got up until noon, but she began whimpering with the birds. After she'd got Myrtle aroused, she would mercifully shut up for a little, while she had her rub and her tray, but directly this was over, she'd start in again, whimpering for Mrs. Cugat. She adored Mrs. Cugat — had from the moment she'd laid eyes on her. Mrs. Cugat had become the only person who could soothe her when she felt an attack coming on and as she was liable to an attack every time she had a dull moment, Mrs. Cugat was beginning to bead with sweat at the sound of her voice. And she called Mrs. Cugat 'Betty.' 'What do they call you, dear?' she had asked sweetly that first night over her tomato soup, and Mrs. Cugat, answering 'Liz,' had been horrified to have Cousin Adela cry, 'No, no! I want to call you Betty!' and stick to it. Mrs. Cugat had been called 'Liz' all her life and being called 'Betty' made her crawl. But that made no difference to Cousin Adela. When the impending attack was soothed, Cousin Adela would then embark upon a salt spray or a mud bath or a series of electric shocks to give her tone. They gave Mrs. Cugat, mercifully, a brief interlude before lunch in which to do the ordering and most of the house-work. Also to deal with the problem of Leonard's inroads on Mr. Cugat's Scotch, Cousin Adela's inroads on Mr. Cugat's brandy, and the laundress thinking she ought to know that there were sixty-four bath towels in the wash that week. It was the only time she had for such details because in the after-noon Cousin Adela liked to go driving. They had been every afternoon — affectionately holding hands in the rear seat of the station-wagon while Leonard, in his béret, steered drowsily, and not always very straight, up one street and down another. They occasionally passed intimates of Mrs. Cugat's who almost fell out of their cars with curiosity, but Mrs. Cugat simply stared stonily ahead. Cousin Adela never wanted to go any-where or see anybody, she just liked to get Mrs. Cugat by the hand, where she couldn't get away, and talk. Mrs. Cugat had politely talked back for a while, asking sympathetically about what's-his-name in India and what Adela's plans for the babies were, but she'd given it up. Any reference to what's-his-name invariably brought on an attack (Adela hated to say it about the babies' own father, but he was a perfect swine) and any mention of the babies brought on tears — of maternal tender-ness, presumably. All in all, it seemed safer to just let Adela do the talking. She wanted to, anyway.

The babies, meanwhile, roamed the house — taking show-ers, changing their nail polish, making cocoa, and playing the victrola. Usually *Tchaikowsky's Piano Concerto in B Flat* on REPEAT. Mrs. Cugat had to admit they were rather sweet, but they seemed too big for a house — like Great Danes. They couldn't be in a room half an hour without filling every ashtray. She felt she ought to get around to doing something about them — take them over to the club where there was more room and introduce them to somebody their own size or something — but so far she simply hadn't had time to do any-thing but hold Adela's hand and stave off domestic dissolution.

That afternoon Mr. Cugat called from the office when he got in from Washington, but Mrs. Cugat was, as usual, out driving. Anna, however, broke her silence to report, when she got back, that he was well and bringing Mr. Cartwright out to dinner. Anna sounded almost cheerful — evidently sensing rescue. Mrs. Cugat, feeling much the same, flew around setting the table — for five (Cousin Adela ate her proteins on a tray in the evening) — and sweeping up the babies' afternoon's accumulation of ashes. Maybe, she thought wistfully, if she waited until the last minute, there'd be a chance of *her* getting a shower. She hadn't had one for four days — Cousin Adela's bathroom being rigged up with everything but an iron lung and the babies always in theirs. She hurried upstairs. They were in there now, steam coming through the keyhole, water seeping under the door. Taking off her clothes, she lay down on the bed to wait.

Refreshingly deep-toned voices, rising from the vestibule, awakened her. 'Just dump your bag there —'; 'You wash up, I'll make a drink —'; 'Shall we have a cocktail or a —' Then the voices stopped abruptly.

'I say, who are you?' one of the babies was heard to ask after a long moment.

'Who are *you*?' said Cory's startled voice. 'Madeleine Carroll?'

The babies laughed. 'One of them's Cousin George!' the other baby exclaimed; adding charmingly, 'You did fool us! We thought you'd be *old*!'

Mrs. Cugat hurried into her clothes.

She got downstairs to find the babies enchanting in long white organdie, the *Piano Concerto* going full blast, and Mr. Cugat mixing martinis. One baby danced demurely in Cory's reverent arms, the other prettily waited upon Mr. Cugat with a tray. 'Well, hel-lo!' said Mr. Cugat, turning to greet her, voice lilting with youth. Cousin Adela, in grey chiffon with sweet peas in her hair and no idea whatever of eating proteins on a tray, swept in.

'George, my pet!' she exclaimed vivaciously, 'it seems like yesterday!'

'Not to me,' said Mr. Cugat, giving the babies a look; 'there wasn't anything like this around yesterday!'

Dinner was positively frolicsome. Mrs. Cugat watched Cousin Adela with glum incredulity. She was charming and gracious and gay. She never whimpered once. She told Mr. Cugat how lovely his wife was, how beautifully his house ran, and how fond she'd always been of him. Blood, she reminded him, with a little catch in her voice, was, after all, thicker than water, as his hospitality had proved. Mr. Cugat reddened and said to think nothing of it. Cory, enraptured with the babies, rose to unprecedented heights of nonsense and showed every sign of falling heels over head in love with both of them at once. And the babies were provocative and adorable. They recited naughty limericks with deliciously charming naïveté and asked grave, innocent questions. After dinner they got everybody into a ridiculous game called 'You and Who Else,' and then turned on the victrola and taught Cory and Mr. Cugat the Bumps-a-Daisy. They modestly but intelligently discussed every known outdoor sport from skiing to salmon fishing, and knew the names of all the ranking American tennis players. Did they play golf, Cory asked hopefully. Oh, rather! Of sorts. One baby played in the high seventies, the other in the low eighties. Well! How about a foursome, then, tomorrow — Mr. Cugat and the baby who played in the eighties against Cory and the baby who played in the seventies? Mr. Cugat looked nothing loath, certainly. 'Lovely!' applauded Cousin Adela, clapping her hands.

'How about you, Liz?' Mr. Cugat asked, in frank afterthought.

'Betty and I are going driving tomorrow, aren't we, darling?' interjected Cousin Adela with the faintest suggestion of a whimper. (She hadn't forgotten how, then.) She bit a trembling lip. 'We have such lovely times together — I couldn't bear to be disappointed!' Mrs. Cugat patted her hand — out of habit — and Mr. Cugat, reassured, began planning some badminton for Monday. 'You don't know,' sighed Cousin Adela to Cory, 'what it means to me to have found George again. Someone to lean on — someone to help with the babies!'

'Nice work if you can get it, eh, George?' burbled Cory. Mr. Cugat grinned foolishly.

'Why, the old — *goats!*' muttered Mrs. Cugat.

Slapping on cleansing cream in front of the somewhat murky mirror of her childhood, she heard Mr. Cugat lock the front door and ascend the stairs. 'Good night, Adela!' he called cheerily, on his way down the hall.

'Dear George!' said Cousin Adela, popping out before the words were out of his mouth.

'Got everything to make you comfortable?' inquired Mr. Cugat thoughtfully.

'Everything!' she cooed. 'How can we ever thank you?'

'There's nothing to thank us for,' protested Mr. Cugat, 'we ought to thank you for livening up the place. Liz gets pretty lonesome, you know —'

'Dear little Betty!'

Mrs. Cugat put down the cleansing cream and gripped the bureau.

'What are your plans?' he continued practically.

Cousin Adela sighed. 'There are times,' she said, 'when I scarcely know — but the d'Abruzzis want us to come to them in Palm Beach after Christmas —'

'What's worrying you, then,' said Mr. Cugat; 'stay with us for Christmas, of course!'

'Dear George,' she whimpered. 'Bless you!'

'Sleep tight,' adjured Mr. Cugat and, whistling lightly, came on down the hall.

4

AND HUMOR THY MOTHER-IN-LAW

Are you mad at something?' queried Mrs. Cugat.

Mr. Cugat looked up from his plate, eyes clouded with abstraction. 'Mad?' he said vaguely. 'No. Why?'

'Well, you've hardly spoken all through dinner. I thought maybe I'd said something —'

'No. Just one or two things on my mind,' he apologized.

'Business?'

'Uh-huh.'

'Why don't you tell me?' she suggested sympathetically. 'When I have things on my mind, I always find that discussing them with you helps a lot.'

Mr. Cugat smiled. 'It's nothing important,' he said, 'just a lot of little run-of-the-mill problems.'

'Tell me, anyway.'

He rose, lit a cigarette, stretched and sauntered toward the library, propelling Mrs. Cugat along ahead of him by the back of her neck. 'You'd be bored to death,' he said.

'I wouldn't. I might be able to help, even.'

'All right, then — old Lady Bonwit wants me to sell her governments and buy rails.'

'Is that bad?'

'I don't like it. I can't imagine who's been talking to her — unless that good-for-nothing nephew has shown up again. She'll never listen to anything I say when he's in town.' Mrs. Cugat clucked indignantly. 'Then, we got an adverse decision handed down in the Probate Court this morning on the Stone estate case —'

'You didn't!' expostulated Mrs. Cugat. 'What's the Stone estate case?'

'A long dull story,' said Mr. Cugat glumly, and went on, 'Two of our best tellers received notifications from their draft boards today and the only girl in the Savings Department who knows anything at all says she's going to quit and have a baby.'

'It must be very hard to get experienced people now, too,' said Mrs. Cugat, feeling that she was not being very much help.

'It's impossible,' he said shortly, and sank into his chair, put his head back and closed his eyes. 'Your mother was in this morning,' he said, after a moment.

'Oh goodness!' exclaimed Mrs. Cugat guiltily, 'I've been meaning to call her all day. What did she want?'

'She wants to open the Palm Beach house again,' he said wearily. 'Now, of all times! I had to tell her she couldn't.'

'Poor darling,' crooned Mrs. Cugat, stroking his hair, 'was she difficult?'

'No-o-o. She's never difficult. She just looks disappointed. You know,' he said, getting suddenly to his feet and starting to walk up and down, 'it's very embarrassing for me — having to manage her affairs. Every time I won't let her spend a lot of money on some fool thing, I always feel that she thinks I'm trying to save it for — us.'

'Oh, I don't believe she thinks that!' protested Mrs. Cugat.

'I don't know — I feel funny about it. I wish somebody else would take her over.'

'You'd have a fit if they did,' said Mrs. Cugat. 'You know you're proud of the way you've managed Daddy's estate — people are always mentioning it. Don't pay any attention to Mother — she's just one of those old-fashioned women who don't know what life is all about.' Mr. Cugat sighed. 'The trouble with the women of her generation,' went on Mrs. Cugat, warming to her subject, 'is that they were brought up to be just — orchids.'

'You take taxes, now,' put in Mr. Cugat worriedly. 'I tell her they're going to eat up nearly half of her income this year and she seems to be listening — but she goes right on living as usual.' Mrs. Cugat shook her head. 'She couldn't understand why I wouldn't let her heat the greenhouse this winter and now she wants to go to Florida!'

'Poor old Mother,' said Mrs. Cugat sadly.

'I suppose when women reach her age,' opined Mr. Cugat, 'they should have some interesting project to keep their minds occupied like — a girls' club or something. Look at Aunt Edith — she seems to get along without all this running around the country!'

'She's a more modern type,' explained Mrs. Cugat.

'Maybe you could point out to your mother,' he suggested, 'that things have changed since her time?'

'I'll have a talk with her,' said Mrs. Cugat firmly.

Opportunity for this was afforded almost immediately, but, somehow, not a great deal came of it.

'Yoo-hoo! Shall I come up?' Mrs. Cugat's mother called from the foot of the stairs, the very next morning.

'Sit down somewhere — I'll be right down,' answered Mrs. Cugat, who was putting away laundry. How did her mother — always so exquisitely put together — manage to get out and around this early in the morning? She never had to sort laundry, of course. She had managed to retain, somehow, a lot of old retainers who asked nothing more of life than to work their fingers to the bone for her.

'Do you know, Anna,' Mrs. Cugat could hear her saying down in the hall, 'I think you must have a special knack with

54

your gingersnaps. What is it you do? Ours are never half so good.'

'Is that right, Mrs. Elliot?' said Anna, and Mrs. Cugat could tell from upstairs that she was grinning from ear to ear. (For the first time in three weeks, incidentally. Anna was congenitally dour.) 'How about me making a batch and sending them over? I'd sure like to.' Mrs. Cugat wagged her head; for one reason or another, Anna had been getting out of gingersnaps all winter. She closed the linen closet and descended to the living-room.

Her mother was standing before a low bookcase propping up a small water-color — a pair of mallards in flight against a grey sky. As expected, she looked exceedingly smart and had a fresh flower in her buttonhole. 'Hello, darling,' she said, turning. 'I saw this picture down at Welbein's yesterday and thought it looked like your room. What have you done to your hair?'

'I didn't have time to wash it yesterday. It looks awful, doesn't it,' said Mrs. Cugat, kissing her.

'A little dull. Are you trying to wash it yourself again? I'd better arrange for some treatments for you at Paul's. You can't go neglecting your hair.'

'Oh, would you!' Mrs. Cugat said gratefully. 'That would be swell.' At a price, Paul, in two short hours, transformed one utterly. 'That picture is perfect there,' she said, enchanted. 'George will love it.'

'I saw George yesterday,' said her mother, stepping off to study the mallards with her head on one side. 'He looked a little tired, I thought.'

Mrs. Cugat cleared her throat. 'He said — you were talking of opening Casa Miranda,' she began.

'I was, but he dashed my hopes completely,' her mother returned cheerfully. 'George, I'm afraid,' she said, with a little laugh, 'considers me a flighty old woman.' Mrs. Cugat said nothing and her mother cocked a quizzical eyebrow at her. 'Do you know,' she observed amusedly, 'he still calls me Mrs. Elliot —'

'Well, you always said,' protested Mrs. Cugat, 'that you hoped he'd never take to calling you "Mother Elliot" like some sons-in-law do —'

'Did I? I don't care for it. I wonder — since I can't go to Florida, maybe I'll take a job in a defense plant — or learn to ice skate —'

'Mother,' said Mrs. Cugat ponderously, 'why don't you get interested in some — project — to — to occupy your mind?'

'Like what?'

'Like Aunt Edith's girls' club — or something.'

'Darling, why don't you?' said her mother pertly. 'Well, I must be off. Don't forget my gingersnaps, Anna!' she called from the front door and, with a gay wave, was gone. Mrs. Cugat sighed, troubled.

It was to be a troubled week. Mr. Cugat came home the following night, looking even more harassed. 'What is it, now?' she asked anxiously. He didn't answer her immediately, but went to the pantry and poured himself a stiff drink.

'Well,' he said, coming back and sinking wearily into his chair, 'I had lunch with Bert Leveret this noon —'

'Yes?' Bert Leveret was the president of the Atlas Sheet Metal and Tool — a staunch concern, at present employing a good half the local citizenry for the manufacture of naval armor plate.

'He says' — Mr. Cugat cleared his throat painfully — 'that your mother was in to see him today.' Mrs. Cugat looked merely inquiring. 'She hit him for a job,' Mr. Cugat finished soberly.

'A *job!* What on earth —'

'He says she wants to run a drill press.'

Mrs. Cugat sat down suddenly. 'She meant it then —'

'Why, did she say anything to you about it?'

'Yes, she did — but I didn't pay any attention. George, we can't *let* her!'

'Bert was terribly embarrassed — took time off from an important meeting to come and see me. He tried to talk her out of it, he said, but she had all his arguments stopped cold. Seems he's advertised for a hundred woman welders and he says he's damned if she probably couldn't do it — but Bert's sort of an old-fashioned guy, you know, and he feels that some of those doves on the swing shift might be pretty swift company for your mother.'

'You'll have to talk her out of it,' said Mrs. Cugat flatly.

'I suppose so,' he sighed. And so, after dinner, he picked up his hat and departed, preoccupied and tight-lipped.

'How did she take it?' Mrs. Cugat asked anxiously on his return, a long hour later.

'Very nice,' he said, troubled; 'I felt like a heel.'

'I don't see why! It was the most ridiculous notion I ever heard of.'

'I think I made her see it,' he admitted relievedly.

Mrs. Cugat decided to take matters into her own hands. Her mother obviously needed something to keep her occupied. After all, she admitted fairly, her mother's chief hobby had been her greenhouse and Mr. Cugat had prevailed upon her to close it. He had also prevailed upon her to stay home from Florida — admirable and patriotic moves both; but her mother's in no way insignificant energies needed some outlet. If only she would get interested in something — fitting — like Aunt Edith's girls' club. Or perhaps, a sewing group at the church —

These worthy suggestions carefully prepared for presentation, Mrs. Cugat, next morning sat down at the telephone.

'Hello, dear,' her mother carolled cheerfully with all that old early morning gusto, 'is everything all right?'

'Oh, yes,' said Mrs. Cugat. 'I just wondered if you were in. I thought I'd come over for a minute —'

Her mother paused. 'Oh,' she said, 'perhaps you'd better come this afternoon — I was just leaving for the airport.'

'The *airport?*'

'Yes. Darling, I'm learning to fly!'

'Mother!'

'I know, you think I can't. I thought so, too, at first. But I can. I read a thing in the paper the other day about this new flying school — right on top of Anne Lindbergh's new book — and then, it seemed like Fate, the man who fixes our icebox told me this morning he had a helicopter to sell. They're the coming thing, you know, but he's being drafted and his wife needs the money —'

'Mother,' said Mrs. Cugat shortly, 'I'm going to call George.'

'Oh, dear.'

'Fly!' snorted Mr. Cugat from the office a moment later. 'Well, let her try it — she won't get off the ground. You have to be pretty young to learn to fly, you know. Co-ordination. I'm too old; you're probably too old, even.'

'She's buying a helicopter,' said Mrs. Cugat quickly, 'from her icebox man.' There was a long pause.

'Did you say a *helicopter?*' Mr. Cugat asked finally.

'That's what she said.'

'Holy mackerel!' he breathed softly. 'All right. I'll attend to it right away.'

Mrs. Cugat hung up with a sigh.

'All right?' she asked him when he came home that night.

'I guess so,' he replied abstractedly.

An uneventful day or two passed and then Mrs. Cugat was relieved to note, one afternoon, her mother, demurely coiffed and folding gauze among the Surgical Dressing ladies at Red

Cross Headquarters. Thinking to bolster this pursuit with personal encouragement, she decided to stop and see her the next morning on her way downtown.

Patrick, the butler, let her in and showed her into the morning room past a ruddy gentleman, gripping a derby and obviously cooling his heels with some impatience in the front hall. Her mother was sitting at her desk surrounded by pamphlets and several unfamiliar-looking volumes bound in calf. Her hair was swept up and decorated with little black bows and she was wearing heavy, and entirely new, harlequin spectacles. Who was it she looked like?

'You seem to be busy,' Mrs. Cugat greeted her, interested.

'I'm up to my ears,' said her mother, frowning prettily. 'It's this new Park Improvement Project. Mr. Monahan — did you run into him out in the hall somewhere? — just brought these over. I'm looking into it.'

'Park Improvement?' murmured Mrs. Cugat, uncertainly.

'Yes. Monahan and some other men from the Tenth Ward are interested in it and it looks like a very good thing to *me*. Only the mayor and the council and a lot of old fuddy-duddies down at the city hall won't have anything to do with it. The project needs somebody with a name and leadership and a crusading spirit, Mr. Monahan says, to put it across.' She smiled dazzlingly, if a little self-consciously, and delved into another pamphlet.

Mrs. Cugat was rather impressed. 'Where is the Tenth Ward?' she asked apologetically.

'I don't know, over on the East Side somewhere, I think. All the people I've met from there seem to be very Irish.'

'What will you have to do?' Mrs. Cugat asked doubtfully.

'Oh, hold rallies and make speeches and sign protests and things,' her mother replied airily. 'Mr. Monahan says that recognition for a thing of this scope might very easily lead to the State Senate!'

Mrs. Cugat looked suddenly at the parade of little black bows up the back of her mother's shining head. Clare Boothe Luce, of course.

She left Mr. Monahan of the Tenth Ward being ushered in by Patrick and walked home thoughtfully. Politics. Often, she had heard Mr. Cugat say that if the better classes were only more public-spirited — Her mother always threw herself heart and soul into anything she undertook and she made a very nice speech — she'd heard her at the Garden Club — This might be just the thing —

Mr. Cugat, however, appeared to think otherwise. He hit the ceiling. 'Pat Monahan, did you say?' he exploded. 'Don't you know that that Tenth Ward machine is the worst blot on the administration — the dirtiest bunch of fixers and fat-fryers the town's ever had! Holy Joe! Old Pat must think the millennium's come. Why, he'll bleed your mother white.'

'Oh, dear! What will we do?'

'Something — quick,' said Mr. Cugat, grabbing his hat again and was gone. She was spending a great many evenings alone lately, Mrs. Cugat reflected.

The following proved to be another. Mr. Cugat, sounding a little overcasual, called at noon next day to say that he would not be home for dinner. He'd forgotten to tell her, but it was the day of the annual Bond Club party. 'I won't be late,' he assured her, unconvincingly. Mrs. Cugat put down the telephone glumly. The Bond Club. Was it possible that another year had rolled around? For some reason, Mr. Cugat — ordinarily stable — for the Bond Club invariably blew his top. 'Does me good to get out with the boys once in a while,' he always excused himself comfortably, with no remorse — and Mrs. Cugat supposed he was right. Although, whoever it was who had built up this theory that all work and no play makes Jack a dull boy might have figured out something for Jill too, she thought grumpily, picking up the telephone again to see if she could find another deserted Bond Club wife to keep her company for the evening.

She was unsuccessful in this, and midnight found her, staring into the dark, quaking and wakeful — having spent an absorbed evening with *The Case of the Moaning Mummy*. The house was full, if not of moans, at least of whispers, and the street outside, dark and empty. She turned restlessly and tried to keep her twitching eyelids closed. No use even to start expecting Mr. Cugat for another two hours, at least — if past performances were anything to go by — but with every car that turned into the street, willy-nilly, her eyes flew open. To start listening for him yet was sheerest idiocy! An hour passed. And then another — during which the Louderbacks' maid came home and Charlie Nelson, across the street. Charlie Nelson was also a Bond Club member and was noted for never leaving anywhere until every drop was drunk — the party must be over. Where was Mr. Cugat? Lurid and familiar pictures began to form and fade. Mr. Cugat lying crumpled in a ditch, dismembered beside a railroad track, stark and unidentified in the morgue. She tried to tell herself that this was foolishness, but people's husbands were killed in accidents — every day. Look at the morning papers — look at Harry Gerskin. Mrs. Gerskin had probably been waiting just like this — telling herself not to worry — and then the telephone had rung —

She awoke to find the light on in the dressing-room and Mr. Cugat, all in one piece, carefully getting out of his trousers. By the clock on the table beside her it was four-thirty. Well, really! For a decent, supposedly reasonable man! Mr. Cugat, as usual after a Bond Club party, was having a little trouble with his trousers.

'Maybe if you held onto something,' she suggested, trying not to sound tart. He looked up and smiled distantly. 'Boys will be boys,' she murmured. Not a bit of use to get sarcastic, she reminded herself warningly and closed her eyes. When she opened them again, he was absorbed in arranging his socks and underwear to his liking over the back of a chair. 'How was the party?' she asked politely. Mr. Cugat cleared his throat, opened his mouth, reconsidered, pursed his lips, frowned importantly, and disappeared into the closet from whence he emerged presently wearing an indignant expression and a pair of tennis shoes. 'Your pajamas and slippers are in the bathroom, as always,' she said kindly, and sighed. If she could only stay in the proper mood to tell him a thing or two in the morning when it might do some good, but by morning, to her disappointment, she always found herself inclined just to try and forget the whole matter. One cannot hit a man when he's down, and Mr. Cugat, on such mornings, was apt to be way down.

The next morning being no exception. 'It's twelve o'clock and we're expected at Mother's for lunch,' she announced cruelly, poking her head into the still darkened bedroom on her return from church. Mr. Cugat rose from the tumbled covers without a word, tacked to the window, closed it, and then sat down carefully in the nearest chair, where he remained for some minutes staring at the floor. 'Shall I make you some coffee?' she suggested, pity smiting her.

'Did you say — we were expected over at your mother's?' he whispered.

'In half an hour.' He closed his eyes. 'Coffee?' He nodded.

She took off her hat and gloves and hurried downstairs. It was Anna's day out, but, forewarned, she had left the percolator ready on the dining-room table. Passing through the hall, however, Mrs. Cugat was arrested by the sound of a car out in front. She went to a window. There was a taxi in the driveway and from it was emerging a large and nattily moustached Army officer. She stared while he turned and assisted to alight, a grey-haired woman wearing white gloves and a bunch of artificial violets. To her knowledge, she had never seen either of them in her life. The officer paid the driver and the cab backed into the street and drove away. They crossed the lawn, walking leisurely, toward the front door.

Mrs. Cugat took the stairs three steps at a time. 'Look out the window quick,' she panted to Mr. Cugat, who was tieing his tie very, very slowly before the mirror, 'and see who this is!' He dropped his hands obediently and went to the window — but not quick. 'Do you know?' she urged anxiously as the doorbell pealed. Mr. Cugat stood motionless; then he drew in a long, deep breath and reached a shaking hand for his coat. 'Come down as soon as you can,' he said through tight lips and swayed toward the stairs.

Mrs. Cugat flew to her dressing-table, dabbed on some powder, pulled a comb through her hair, and sped after him. She arrived at the bottom step just as he was opening the front door.

'WELL? GOOD MORNING!' boomed the officer, rocking Mr. Cugat visibly back on his heels. 'GORGEOUS DAY!'

'How-are-you,' said Mr. Cugat, tonelessly.

'MY MOTHER — MR. CUGAT,' the officer again boomed, drawing the woman with the violets forward.

Mr. Cugat bowed wordlessly over her hand.

Mrs. Cugat cleared her throat and came forward. Mr. Cugat turned a deep magenta. 'Mrs. Cugat — Colonel Framblyump — and Mrs. Framblyaw —' he gargled.

'Won't you come in and sit down?' said Mrs. Cugat, looking anxiously at Mr. Cugat and wondering if men under forty ever had strokes. They all went into the living-room.

'What a pretty house!' chirped Mrs. Framblyaw.

'*We* like it,' said Mrs. Cugat. Everybody sat down and a short, strangling silence fell.

'WHAT WEATHER!' the Colonel boomed again.

'Almost *too* warm, though,' protested Mrs. Cugat, alertly watching Mr. Cugat get out a folded handkerchief and blot his brow.

'I hope,' said the Colonel's mother, after another smothering moment, 'we didn't come too early. Your husband neglected to tell Willard just what time you served luncheon.'

Mrs. Cugat's eyes caught Mr. Cugat's in a brief, stunned glance and he bowed his head. Then he cleared his throat. 'Not at all — not at all!' he protested in a loud, unnatural voice, 'just in time!'

'Will you excuse me for a moment?' breathed Mrs. Cugat, rising. He gave her a beseeching look as she edged out of the room — presumedly for forgiveness — and she dashed up the stairs and made for the telephone.

At just the sound of her mother's voice, Mrs. Cugat found herself weak with relief. 'Of course — bring them over,' her mother said calmly. 'I have only four squab, but we'll manage something. What did you say their name is?'

'I don't believe he knows,' breathed Mrs. Cugat.

'Dear me,' said her mother. 'Where did you say he met them?'

'At the Bond Club party, I imagine.'

'Ah.'

Mrs. Cugat hastened back to the living-room. 'It's lucky you came a little early,' she said, entering, bright but shaky. 'Our cook, unfortunately, has just been called away — by illness in her family — so — my mother — has invited us to come over and have luncheon with her — she's *so* anxious to meet you both.' She paused to collect her wits and had an inspiration. 'George, while I'm getting ready, why don't you mix us all a cocktail?' Mr. Cugat, with the look of a dying

man who has just heard penicillin prescribed, leapt to his feet, but the Colonel, with a sidelong look at his parent, hurrumphed gruffly, 'NOTHING FOR ME, THANKS!' and Mr. Cugat sank back.

'We never touch spirits,' explained Mrs. Framblyaw primly.

'Oh. Well, then,' said Mrs. Cugat, crippled but still functioning, 'will you excuse us both for a moment while we put on our things —'

They hurried together up the stairs. '*What* did you say that name was?' she hissed, pushing him into the bedroom and closing the door.

'I don't know,' he muttered, holding his head; 'I can't remember!'

'How did you meet them?' she probed. 'Think!'

'Oh, I know,' he protested dully, 'that he's a Colonel Some-Body-or-Other from Washington who's here looking over the Aetna plant — they must have an Army contract. He was at the party last night and we knocked off a few together. I suppose,' he added contritely, 'I must have asked him to lunch.'

'And told him to be sure and bring his dear old mother,' she finished tersely. Adding with feeling, 'Thank Heaven for mine!'

Her mother was standing in the doorway when they arrived, and Mrs. Cugat knew she had never been so glad to see anyone in her life. She fell upon her with a grateful hug; Mr. Cugat bent to kiss her hair. 'Don't overdo it, dears,' Mrs. Elliot murmured, adding gently, 'I fixed a little something for you, George — it's in the pantry,' and stepped toward her unknown guests with outstretched hands. 'Do you know, Colonel,' she said, aloud, with a charming smile, 'ever since Mary Elizabeth told me you were coming, I've been *wondering* how you spell your name —'

'A-S-K, Ask,' said the Colonel shortly.

'The reason I was wondering,' said Mrs. Cugat's mother without so much as turning a hair and linking her arm cosily in that of Mrs. A-S-K, Ask, 'is that I once knew some Army people who spelled it with — *two* K's. A-S-K-*K*. Very odd — I think they must have been Swedish or something. They were perfectly charming, though,' she added, 'from — Georgia.'

'Why, we're from Georgia,' said the Colonel's mother.

'Yo ah!' exclaimed Mrs. Cugat's mother delightedly. 'Ah wuz bo'n in 'tlantuh!'

'Honey chile! Yew mus' knaow tha Ca'in'tons!'

'Oh, co'se!'

A small world. Everybody joined in exclamations of incredulity — some of them very real. For a Cleveland girl, Mrs. Cugat reflected, her mother got around.

They proceeded into the sunny, flower-filled living-room to be followed almost immediately by Patrick, bearing a tray of Daiquiris. '*They don't drink*,' chanted Mrs. Cugat under her breath.

'A li'l sherbet, Miz Ask?' said her mother, promptly taking a cocktail from the tray and pressing it upon that lady firmly. Miz Ask accepted it graciously, sipped, smiled, and drank deeper.

'Delicious!' she pronounced and the Colonel reached abruptly for a second.

'Mah gran'muthuh's recipe,' said Mrs. Cugat's mother, without a scruple. 'Naow, do tell me, Miz Ask, all '*bout* you-all!'

Miz Ask began to vouchsafe enlightening information; Mrs. Cugat began to relax a little; the Colonel began to stare, spaniel-like, at Mrs. Cugat's mother. Mr. Cugat returned from the pantry, looking a new man, and began to stare, spaniel-like, at her mother too. Luncheon was announced. It proved ample, delicious, and, by the time coffee was served, preposterously Southern. The party broke up, however, quite soon after it was over because of a drowsy spell which unaccountably attacked Miz Ask.

'Really,' said Mrs. Cugat, on their way home, 'you've got to admit that, in her way, mother's remarkable.'

'She's wonderful,' said Mr. Cugat simply; 'we don't see enough of her. You know,' he went on after a moment, 'she must get very lonely all by herself in that big house —'

'Well, she's always travelled a lot, you know — and been busy with the greenhouse — but, of course, that's all out now —' Mr. Cugat looked thoughtful. 'If only she'd see more of your Aunt Edith and get wrapped up in that club of hers —'

'My Aunt Edith is an unmitigated bore,' said Mr. Cugat, surprisingly.

Privately, Mrs. Cugat had always thought so. It really was utterly ridiculous, she realized, suddenly honest, to imagine Aunt Edith and her mother wrapped up in anything together. 'I ought to see more of Mother, myself,' she said, contrite. 'It's probably loneliness that makes her restless. Maybe she'd like to go to those concerts with me —'

'Maybe she would!' said Mr. Cugat, enthusiastically, adding, pleased, 'Then I wouldn't have to!'

Mrs. Cugat, a concert in mind, called her mother the following Tuesday morning. 'Oh, darlin',' her mother exclaimed regretfully, 'Ah'm so sorry, but Ah'm goin' out ag'in wif yo' cuh'nel!'

'*Again?*'

'Dancin',' her mother elucidated.

'Does *he* dance?' stammered Mrs. Cugat stupidly.

'Jus' divine. Ah think he's had lessons.'

'But when —?'

'Wha, Ah had dinnuh wif him on Monday — di'n Ah tell

you-all? We discovuhed a new place called Sambo's. They have real, 'onest-tuh-goo'ness mint juleps!'

'What about Miz Ask?' inquired Mrs. Cugat dazedly.

'Gone back to 'tlantuh,' her mother replied light-heartedly, adding in a more natural tone, 'thank Heaven!'

Astounded, Mrs. Cugat related all this to Mr. Cugat, who appeared equally taken aback. 'Well, I'll be damned!' he said, amused.

Honest-to-goodness mint juleps, however, being nothing to pass up these days, a night or two later found them at Sambo's Bar themselves — a cosy spot, very deep South even to colored mammies and paper magnolias. The food, however, appeared to be strictly Kosher. 'Hello!' said Mr. Cugat, looking out across the room, over his herring, 'if there aren't Scarlet O'Hara and the Colonel again!'

'He's not *still* in town?' exclaimed Mrs. Cugat, craning her neck. 'He's certainly taking his time about looking that plant over!'

'The Aetna people think so,' said Mr. Cugat. 'Charlie Erskin's fit to be tied, they say. He's got a deal on to sell out to somebody, providing they can land this Army contract, but the Colonel's stalling around so, the buyer's going to back out —'

'He's looking positively drooly at Mother!' put in Mrs. Cugat, not taking her eyes off her parent.

'I know,' said Mr. Cugat. 'Old Ask's got a hell of a reputation as a lady's-man.' Then he asked, after a little pause, 'You don't think your mother could be falling for him, do you?'

'At *her* age?' protested Mrs. Cugat.

'How old is she?' he asked, curiously.

'She must be forty-nine!'

Mr. Cugat was silent for a moment. 'That's only ten years older than I am,' he said, in an odd tone. 'How old are you?'

'Twenty-nine,' she said abstractedly, still looking.

Across the room her mother rose to let her gallant hold her coat. It was abloom with orchids. 'You know,' said Mr. Cugat, watching his mother-in-law walk out between the tables, followed by her obviously adoring escort, 'I never noticed her before —'

'You don't think the Colonel could be *really* serious, do you?' Mrs. Cugat asked anxiously, following them with her eyes. Her mother *did* have a cute figure.

'I'd hate to think so,' he said thoughtfully, 'that old boy's *had* three wives —'

'Darling!'

The Colonel caught sight of them, and waved. 'H'lo, you-all!' called his lady unconcernedly.

'Golly!' whispered Mrs. Cugat.

Her next few days were depressingly overcast. Every time she thought of the Colonel, she grew rigid with dislike. The possibility that one day she might have to accept him appalled her. That booming voice! That jaunty angle to his cap! The way he slapped his thigh. She suspected that he waxed his moustache and, rather unjustly, that he wore a girdle. And his name was Willard. She *loathed* the name of Willard! Then, one morning, a long box of roses arrived with, really, quite a charming little note from him. She put them, un-opened, in the icebox and tore the card to bits.

'He's still here!' she announced grimly to Mr. Cugat that evening.

'I know,' he replied soberly, 'and your mother had him with the Atterburys for dinner last night.'

'Oh, my goodness!' she exclaimed, appalled. 'Do you think she's *showing* him to the Atterburys?'

'I don't know,' said Mr. Cugat, who was having the Colonel looked up.

'What will we do?'

Mr. Cugat patted her hand. 'Keep calm,' he said.

Mrs. Cugat decided that someone would have to talk to her mother. But who? Every time she thought of doing it herself, she grew hot with embarrassment. Several days passed in an agony of vacillation, and then, 'Hello!' her mother carolled from the front hall, making another of her early morning calls. 'Are you coming down?'

'Right away,' said Mrs. Cugat, steeling herself. This was it. What on earth could one say?

Her mother was carrying an armful of hothouse daffodils and white stock, had on pale grey flannel under her mink coat and looked like Mary Martin. No wonder she'd caught herself a beau! Had she always looked so young? Mrs. Cugat didn't know, she'd never noticed. 'Aren't these nice?' her mother was saying, 'I love early spring flowers. Do you want me to fix them? A deep glass bowl, I think, Anna,' she said, giving the flowers to Mrs. Cugat and obligingly taking off her gloves. Anna, as usual, sped joyously to do her bidding.

'Mother,' Mrs. Cugat blurted, 'what about the Colonel?'

'Colonel? Oh, thank you, Anna. Let me see, let's put it here on this paper.'

'Colonel Ask.'

'Oh, that colonel.' Her mother took the flowers from her again, and, kneeling down on the floor, spread them out on a newspaper. 'He's gone back to Washington. Mr. Stettinius sent for him. The Bolivians were waiting.'

'Bolivians?'

'Yes. There seems to be some plant here that makes a little thing that just fits their planes. We're being nice to South Americans now, you know, so Mr. Stettinius sent Colonel Ask out here to look into it for them — he knows about such things. He took quite a while about it — only because he wanted to make quite sure it was right — but you know South Americans — hot-headed.'

'When,' said Mrs. Cugat, expelling a long sigh, 'did he leave?'

'Last night,' said her mother brightly. 'These are going to be rather sweet in this blue bowl —'

'Well, let's hope he stays there!' Her mother went on poking the long, thick stems deftly into the bowl, but she began humming a little tune. 'He isn't coming *back*, is he?' Mrs. Cugat asked, in sudden alarm.

'Not that I know of, dear,' said her mother, and added, with a sidelong glance, 'I won't be here, in any case —'

'Where are you going?'

'Florida.'

'But I thought George decided —'

'George has evidently changed his mind,' said her mother, standing up to view her handiwork. 'I'm leaving next week and I'm so pleased. He sent my tickets and reservations over only this morning with a sweet note. I have it here somewhere,' she went on, dipping into her bag. 'Here. George is a darling! And do you know, he's stopped calling me "Mrs. Elliot"!'

Mrs. Cugat took the note and read it. 'Honey chile,' it said, 'Skedaddle!'

5

IDOLS IN CELLULOID

Mrs. Sturm's downstairs,' said Anna laconically, sticking her head into the bathroom. Mrs. Cugat, who was washing out stockings, looked up with a little frown of annoyance which did not lessen as her eyes encountered the figure in the door. Anna, no matter how often she was told, would not remember to tidy herself up before she answered the bell. She was arrayed, now, in a bedraggled uniform, an old pair of patent-leather pumps, pink silk socks, and a green chenille snood. Her skirt was tucked up and she carried a drain plunger.

'Anna! You didn't go to the door like that!' Mrs. Cugat whispered reproachfully — Evie Sturm's door was answered, in the mornings, by an Englishman in an alpaca coat. She dried her hands hurriedly and began to take the curlers out of the ends of her hair. 'I hope you didn't leave her just standing in the hall,' she said, with no confidence, and Anna flushed guiltily. 'Well, never mind, go and tell her I'll be right down.'

Mrs. Howard B. Sturm, III, was discovered, looking exceedingly smart and particularly bright-eyed, in the midst of chaos in the living-room. 'Darling!' she exclaimed, as Mrs. Cugat clambered over the vacuum cleaner and came in, 'I've got the most exciting news!'

'Tell me!' said Mrs. Cugat, hurriedly steering her into the sunroom which appeared to be in a more nearly normal state.

Mrs. Sturm turned, her eyes wide. '*Guess* who we're having for the week-end!'

'The Duke and Duchess of Windsor,' guessed Mrs. Cugat flippantly. Actually, Evie Sturm was quite capable of producing H. R. H. and the Duchess. She was an exasperating person.

'André Moret!' breathed Mrs. Sturm, and stood off to watch it sink in.

Mrs. Cugat blinked. 'You're *not!*' she finally managed.

Mrs. Sturm nodded excitedly. 'Howie,' she explained, 'is on the War Chest Committee, you know. Well, the final rally is next week and that's who the guest speaker is to be! Did you ever hear of such a break?'

'No,' said Mrs. Cugat, and asked with envy, 'And he's staying at your house?' Really, Evie did manage things.

'He is,' said Mrs. Sturm, suddenly serious. 'As soon as I heard about it, I had Howie fix it up to have me put on the committee as Chairman of Entertainment. They had somebody planned you never heard of — the president of the Chamber of Commerce or something. But I got rid of that idea for them. I didn't see any sense in letting a divine person like Moret get all mixed up in flag-raisings and banquets with the mayor. Or worse,' she added, with a gleam, 'fall into the clutches of Thyra Morgan and her crowd. You know, when *she* gets wind of him, what will happen — she'll be on my trail. So I'm going to get every minute of his time arranged today. She'll probably be furious, but it's about time those old hags retired — there's hardly one of them under thirty-five!'

'What have you planned?' asked Mrs. Cugat, when she could get a word in.

'That's what I want to talk to you about,' said Mrs. Sturm briskly, and produced a paper and pencil from her bag. 'They said he probably wouldn't get here until late Friday afternoon,' she proceeded, 'so that means the only free time he'll have will be Friday night after the Rally and on Saturday. I thought I'd see if you wouldn't like to have a late supper on Friday — you always have such cute parties — and then I'll have something Saturday noon, around the pool. What do you think of that?' Mrs. Cugat was pleased and extremely flattered. 'We won't have everybody,' Mrs. Sturm went on earnestly — 'just *insiders*. I've got a list here, all made out.'

Mrs. Cugat examined it and counted the names. 'Yes,' she said, 'but I'll have to ask George, first, if he wants to. Can I let you know tomorrow?'

'Tomorrow! Darling, we've got to get everything planned *today* on account of that Morgan bitch. For goodness' sakes, don't tell me you consult George about parties! I never do Howie. Men always want to have funny people and make a complete mess of things.'

'I know,' admitted Mrs. Cugat, 'but I think maybe, in this case, I'd better.'

'You can't!' said Mrs. Sturm emphatically. 'He might say "no," and, as a matter of fact,' she added, a little guiltily, 'I've already told Thyra that she *couldn't* have a party for him Friday night because you *were*. I *had* to, darling. I was desperate. She was insistent — pretending they'd known each other in Biarritz and I don't know what all. Wouldn't you think, at her age —'

Light broke in on Mrs. Cugat. So that was it! Just Evie and Thyra hair-pulling over another man. And she being high-handedly made use of by Evie because Evie, quite evidently, considered her harmless. So steeped in domesticity that she was incapable of making an even mildly dangerous impression on 'the Gable of Gaul.' Well! Her first reaction — to decline with a few coldly caustic remarks — was suddenly supplanted by affronted vanity crying for vengeance. She'd teach Miss Evie a thing or two! Just because she happened to be reasonably fond of her own husband didn't mean she was completely on the shelf. Evie was probably counting on her to wear a last year's summer dress and serve ice cream and cake on the front porch — the perfect foil for a parade of hostess pajamas and French seventy-fives around the swimming pool. Ha ha! 'If that's the way it is,' she said, ominously gentle, 'of course, I'll do it. I can manage George all right. Let's see that list again.'

During the next few days she resolutely marshalled her forces. Her annoyance had somewhat cooled and a qualm or two set in. Evie, with her neo-French farmhouse, English butler, and hundred-foot pool, was something to compete with. The thing to do, of course, was simply to forget these and plan the most delightful party possible in her own setting. She considered it soberly. Evie's list had consisted of about twenty-five to thirty names, which, however select, in the Cugats' neo-Cape Cod cottage was a lot too many. Unless, of course, she used the terrace. The terrace wasn't very big, but it opened off the dining-room, through French doors, was prettily banked with shrubbery and faced a small rectangle of grass with what had once been a pond of goldfish in its centre. The pond was long since dry and full of leaves, and nothing about the terrace furniture suggested Hollywood, certainly, being ancient wicker with flaking paint, but both these could be remedied. It was high time they did something about the terrace, anyway. Nobody ever used it, and small wonder. Casting prudence to the winds, she went downtown and invested in two white iron chairs and a settee. This had such a miraculously transforming effect that her enthusiasm broke into flame and she went back and got a double chaise-longue with an awning and a portable bar on rubber-tired wheels. Then she had the inside of the goldfish pond painted blue and installed four goldfish. The difference was indescribable!

There was one worrisome detail, however. As a setting for a bang-up supper party, both terrace and garden were going to be pretty woodsy and dim. The lights from the dining-room, turned on full, seemed to penetrate hardly at all and the calendar promised no moon. She racked her brain, experimented with hurricane lamps, and finally decided again to hang the expense and call in an electrician to investigate the feasibility of (Heaven forbid!) Japanese lanterns. The man who came, as luck would have it, turned out to be something of a genius — a fledgling Jo Mielziner, apparently. He offered, nonchalantly, to put up a moon. A little invention of his own and very successful. In the cold light of day this innovation proved to be a distressingly expensive and ugly yellow disk mounted on a prominent iron pole, strung with wires and flanked by bug lamps. But at night its effect was magical. It transformed the terrace and garden into a little stage. The clapboards of the house gleamed white, the syringa jade green, the pond splintered silver. Mrs. Cugat, in exaltation at what she had wrought, went down and bought a new dress of billowing grey organdie splashed with stars and a silver bird for her hair. The scene was set.

On the Tuesday before the great day, however, she was sitting under the drier at the hairdresser's thumbing through a movie magazine when she came upon this: *Moret. Bull-shouldered Idol of the Boulevards. The New Menace. Would rather Cook than Make Love! See recipes, p. 14.* Above which was a picture of M. Moret, very debonnaire in a chef's cap and apron.

'What's this?' inquired Mr. Cugat the next evening, peering suspiciously into the steaming tureen that Anna had just put before him.

'Bouillabaisse,' replied Mrs. Cugat offhandedly. 'Remember it in France?'

'I guess so. Aren't we getting a little fancy?'

Anna looked eloquent.

'Not at all,' Mrs. Cugat said crisply. 'It's a very simple recipe, really. I just happened to run across it and thought I'd try it out in case we want to use it for a party sometime.'

Mr. Cugat took a cautious mouthful. 'Fish,' he said.

Anna looked compassionate. 'How about me fixing you a nice egg?' she whispered.

Mrs. Cugat's mouth set. 'That won't be necessary, Anna,' she said; 'go get the stuffed mushrooms.'

Mr. Cugat chewed languidly. 'The final War Chest Rally is next week,' he remarked, sparring for time between bites.

Mrs. Cugat colored. Rightly or wrongly she had not yet told Mr. Cugat about the supper party — and the longer she let it go, the harder it seemed to get. Every day there was more to explain. She cleared her throat. 'Evie said something —' she began unhappily.

'They tried to get me to serve on the Entertainment Committee,' went on Mr. Cugat, taking a long drink of water, 'but I told them "nothing doing."' Then he added cheerfully, 'They've got some movie star or other coming.'

'Yes,' said Mrs. Cugat. 'Why didn't you want to serve?'

'Haven't got the time and I need my sleep,' he asserted briefly. 'This going back and forth to Washington every other week with the old man, trying to keep up with my regular work and soliciting subscriptions, is tough enough without staying out all night at a lot of parties. There are plenty of others — ready to jump at it.'

'Oh dear,' she murmured, 'I should have known!' Mr. Cugat looked up alertly. 'I'm afraid I didn't think — I got you into a little something, I guess.' She wet her lips. 'Evie came over and was insistent, and I thought, after all — just a little supper party. In times like these, we all ought to do all we can, don't you think? And the terrace really looks so much better! If you want to, you can give it all to me for my birthday —'

'Come again?' said Mr. Cugat gently, putting down his spoon.

'Our new terrace furniture,' she explained with a fine semblance of nonchalance. 'Come out and look!'

Mr. Cugat, hands in his pockets, walked around the garden and hummed. Eagerly, she demonstrated the bar, opened the awning on the chaise-longue and, tremulous, turned on the moon. 'How much?' he said at length.

An entirely spurious and comparatively meagre figure rose to her lips and, incredibly, popped out. How, she couldn't imagine. She had had no intention of lying to him. Mr. Cugat closed his eyes. Then he turned and went back to the dining-room. She joined him apprehensively. 'It isn't as if we hadn't been needing it for a long time —' she began.

'Could Anna fry me a couple of eggs?' he asked quietly.

Mrs. Cugat hurriedly rang the bell. 'The supper party is just going to be a simple little affair, really — and after all, it isn't every day you get the opportunity to entertain someone like André Moret.'

'Who's he?'

'Oh, George — that's the movie star! — Mr. Cugat would like two fried eggs, Anna — That's who the party's *for*.'

'*What's* his name?'

'Moret. Good Lord, George, haven't you even heard of him? He's the new French actor that everybody's raving about!'

Mr. Cugat looked unimpressed, but cheered visibly as Anna bounced triumphantly back in with a simmering plate.

'When's all this going to be?' he asked, bending down for a gratified sniff.

78

'Day after tomorrow —'

'Well, you'll have to count me out,' he said cheerfully. 'I've got to get a report out that night.'

Mrs. Cugat sighed and let it pass. Passive resistance could be dealt with later. Anxiously, she sampled the cold bouillabaisse.

Under flag-draped girders and hot white lights, the War Chest Rally was about to begin. The auditorium was packed, the band played *Anchors Aweigh*, the mayor was on his feet, ready to go. Sitting on the platform were to be seen assorted and bemedalled representatives of the armed forces, coiffed and capped representatives of the Red Cross, earnest members of the Junior League, and smiling incumbents of the city hall. A gigantic thermometer for the purpose of registering the progress of pledges rose at the back of the stage with a Boy Scout bugle corps drawn up at its base.

Mrs. Cugat, with a decidedly Parisian upswept hair-do but outwardly composed, was down in front. Mr. Cugat, however, was not with her. He had remained adamant to the last and was at home closeted with his report. 'It's going to be terribly hard to explain,' she had protested. 'It makes you look so — unpatriotic!' Mr. Cugat, who had spent about fifty per cent of his nights, during the past six months, on the Washington sleeper and a good fifty per cent of his days for the past week soliciting War Chest subscriptions, had merely glared. However, to make up, he had arranged to have the best bartender at the club out to help with the drinks and generously produced a case of rum. Mrs. Cugat had hoped to serve nothing but champagne, but found she was able to afford only three bottles on her own and pry but three more from her mother's butler, so a case of rum, however plebeian, was certainly going to come in handy. For what must have been the hundredth time that day, she went over in her mind each small detail and, at length, settled back in her seat, content.

The mayor adjusted the microphone, rattled his notes, and a hush fell. 'Ladies and gentlemen,' he began in Titan tones, and smiled benevolently over the audience, 'we have an unexpected treat in store for you tonight —' There was an impressive pause, filled with still expectancy, and His Honor cleared his throat and adjusted his glasses. 'The Committee has asked me to announce,' he went on, bowing to the Committee, who stared back woodenly, 'that, due to a stroke of good luck, they are able to bring to you tonight, to aid in this great undertaking, a man who needs no introduction; a man whose career each one of us here has followed proudly; whose daring and bravery has been unexcelled! And who, when our call came, answered that call. I can see by your faces that I need say no more. My friends, I am happy, nay proud, to welcome, in-place-of-the-speaker-expected-this-evening-who-has-been-unavoidably-detained-in-the-East, this city's contribution to Hollywood, our own — Walter Ganch!' The band struck up *Anchors Aweigh* again, the doors at the back of the auditorium burst open, and a detachment of marines marched smartly in. Walter Ganch, a muscular little man with kinky hair and a plaid sport coat, marched in their midst, but Mrs. Cugat, turning dazedly, saw that Mrs. Sturm, who had elected herself (dressed in Motor Corps uniform) to accompany Moret down the aisle, was nowhere to be seen.

The crowd of some two thousand, apparently Ganch fans all, roared in welcome, and their idol reddened, ducked his head, and waved modestly. 'A great guy!' vouchsafed a brawny gentleman next to Mrs. Cugat, noting her apparent stupor. Didn't she know him? One of Hollywood's best stunt men. Did she know the Bijou Sport Palace down on Front Street? His brother, Louis, ran it. A swell place. Swell people. Old circus family. She must remember the

Flying Ganches! Mr. Ganch climbed to the platform and made an earnest and excellent speech, and the audience, who evidently, with the sole exception of Mrs. Cugat, all remembered the Flying Ganches, responded vociferously. Then the Boy Scout bugle corps came forward, rendered an ear-splitting *Boots and Saddles*, and the sale began.

It was a tremendous success. Girl Scouts flitted back and forth bearing pledges, quotas from factories were announced from the floor, an all-girl choir sang *Johnnie Doughboy Found a Rose in Ireland*, and the red line on the giant thermometer grew taller and taller until, at length, to an inspirited roll of drums, it spurted past the quota mark and the roof nearly blew off with the roar of exultation.

'Howie,' breathed Mrs. Cugat, squeezing her grey organdie at last through the milling crowd to where Mr. Sturm was standing beside the platform, '*where is Evie?*'

'Home with a bad headache,' muttered Mr. Sturm, not meeting her eye.

A delegation of what might be aldermen came up and shook him by the hand. 'Congratulations, Howard,' they said jovially, 'a fine job! What's next on the program? We thought it'd be nice to give old Walter a real old-fashioned homecoming tonight.'

Mr. Sturm gave Mrs. Cugat a fleeting look. 'Sure!' he said, clapping the spokesman on the back. 'We're taking him over to George Cugat's now — you know George — vice-president of the Tri-State Trust — he'll be tickled to death to have you! Meet his wife —' Mrs. Cugat, speechless, shook hands. The invitation was accepted with enthusiasm. 'I'm sorry, Liz,' Howie murmured, hustling her along after the flying wedge formation that the political gentlemen were using to get through the crowd; 'I couldn't do anything else. You can't make pink teas out of these affairs, you know. Evie can never understand — but you're a star to stick with it!'

81

They caught up with Walter and the marines at the door. Amid the glare of flash bulbs and the click of cameras, Mrs. Cugat, grey organdie and all, was boosted into a jeep beside him. The marines fell in, a band struck up, and they moved off. Howie, ahead in a flag-draped Packard, waved in grinning encouragement. But it was a long trip. By the end of it Mrs. Cugat found herself bowing and smiling and lifting her hand with all the finish of a Roosevelt.

Like everybody else in the block, Mr. Cugat was peering out of his front door when the jeep pulled to the curb in front of the house. Walter triple-somersaulted to the ground, the marines formed a hasty guard of honor, and Mrs. Cugat alighted. Howie hastened up the front walk and everyone fell briskly into step.

Mr. Cugat came out onto the porch and squinted into the gloom. 'Walter *Ganch* — you old son-of-gun!' he exclaimed suddenly.

'Hiya, George!' said Mr. Ganch, pushing through to clasp both Mr. Cugat's hands in his own. 'It's been a long time, eh, fella?'

'Well, for Pete's sake, come in, come in!' cried Mr. Cugat delightedly. He peered over Howie's shoulder into the crowd. 'Hello, Foley! Hello, Dubinsky! Hel*lo*, Ike!' he greeted the political gentlemen.

The original party — Evie's select list of 'insiders' — trickled in, but were soon lost in the shuffle, there being only thirty of them. The bouillabaisse, stuffed mushrooms, and champagne, needless to say, vanished during the first five minutes. Three times Mr. Cugat sent out for hamburgers and beer, but at 3 A.M. people were still eating.

Wearily climbing the stairs to her room to pin up a few torn flounces — Foley, Ike, and Dubinsky loved to dance — Mrs. Cugat paused at a window which overlooked the garden. What was left of the band was still playing fitfully and two

dreamy couples still waltzed on the terrace. Someone had pulled the double chaise-longue out of the moonlight into the syringa and discreetly lowered the awning. Foley was in the fish pond. Mr. Ganch, surrounded by a cheering throng, was standing on his hands atop a swaying tower of white iron furniture.

Mr. Cugat did not look very well at breakfast and was silent. Mrs. Cugat opened the French doors, gave the terrace a quick look, shuddered, and hastened into the pantry to turn off the moon.

'That was quite a party we had last night,' he said at length above the clatter of his spoon against his coffee cup.

'Yes, wasn't it,' she replied evenly.

'Where were Evie and her Frog?' he asked, in sudden recollection.

Mrs. Cugat did not reply. She was looking at the front page of the noon paper whereon excellent likenesses of herself and Walter in the jeep were prominently displayed.

Mr. Cugat rose and peered over her shoulder. 'Holy Mike!' he exclaimed softly.

'Well, let me remind you that you didn't look any too dignified learning to walk on your hands at four o'clock this morning!' snapped Mrs. Cugat defensively. 'The neighbors must have loved it! We'll probably be asked to move. What a party!' she finished disgustedly.

'That party wasn't my idea,' said Mr. Cugat quietly.

'No,' she gulped, close to tears, 'and it wasn't mine either. I was going to have a perfectly beautiful party — which you, incidentally, refused to have any part of until your acrobatic friend turned up to spoil everything. Where'd you ever know him, anyway?'

'Walter?' exclaimed Mr. Cugat. 'Why, honey, everybody used to know Walter. He was the hero of every kid at State

Street School. He could do anything! I wish, sometime, you could just see him hang by his heels —'

'If you don't mind,' she cut in bitterly, 'I've seen about all of him I can take.'

Mr. Cugat departed for the office and she wearily set about putting the terrace to rights. In about half an hour, however, he telephoned her. 'Ganch is giving a cocktail party at the Statler this afternoon, honey,' he said, 'and wanted me to call and ask you to come.'

'Thank you, no,' said Mrs. Cugat disagreeably. 'I've had enough of acrobats.'

'You gals!' said Mr. Cugat disgustedly. 'Evie turned him down too. Well, better not wait dinner — I may be a little late.'

'Watch your hernia on that back-flip!' retorted Mrs. Cugat tartly, and hung up.

It was very late when Mr. Cugat came in, but he looked ten years younger than he had that morning — his tan was ruddy and his hair stuck up in little curls. 'Did you have a nice day?' he asked solicitously, bending over the bed to kiss her.

'Lovely,' she said, through the fumes of Scotch, 'I washed eight dozen dirty glasses. It's twelve o'clock — that must have been quite a cocktail party.'

'It was, it was,' he said, going to a mirror to look at himself. Mrs. Cugat looked at him too. His eyes were alight and his eyebrows cocked like a satyr's.

'Who was there?' she asked suddenly.

'Honey, it's just a shame you didn't go,' he said earnestly, smoothing down his hair and straightening his tie. 'Walter was awfully disappointed — he wanted you to meet some friends of his who came in on a plane this afternoon.'

'Fellow artists, no doubt?'

84

'Well, yes,' he said. 'A bunch of the cast from his new picture —'

'What's its name this time?' she asked, yawning. Mr. Cugat cleared his throat. 'Well?'

'Sweater Girls in Swing-Time,' he said, grinning.

6

NOR HIS MAIDSERVANT,
NOR HIS MANSERVANT

By NO STRETCH of the imagination could Anna, the Cugats' cook, ever be referred to as 'a jewel' — being casual, ungifted, and impervious to suggestion — but there was one thing Mrs. Cugat could say for her, she was *loyal*. Mrs. Cugat had been saying this for Anna for about five years and, it would seem, had reason to believe it. The blow, consequently, when it fell, was stunning. Without preamble, and right in the middle of lunch, one day, Anna announced that she was going to work in a defense plant! Mrs. Cugat, shaken, tendered a rash and unpremeditated raise, but the gesture was only pathetic. Anna's girl-friend, Clara — a spot welder — it seemed, got that much in a day. And what 'that dumb Clara' could get, Anna could, certainly! She would, however, stay a few days until Mrs. Cugat found somebody. No, she didn't know of anyone, herself. There were plenty of good places open, she guessed; in fact, several of Mrs. Cugat's own friends had spoken to her, but she was done with housework.

Anxiously, Mrs. Cugat called the Employment Bureau. The Employment Bureau laughed — but said they would take her name.

Touchingly, Anna proceeded to devote her last days to unparalleled service. Unbidden, she washed woodwork, cleaned the icebox, and polished silver. She darned up all of Mr. Cugat's socks and swept out the garage — disputed territory.

86

Not once did she flounce to the front door, carrying a mop or with flour on her hands, and she introduced one or two little refinements that had to be seen to be believed — such as pressing Mrs. Cugat's nightgown and pinking the edge of Mr. Cugat's grapefruit. By the end of the week, her every short-coming forgotten and wearing gardenias, she departed in a taxi to be forever honored and forever mourned.

Mrs. Cugat, somewhat spent by the parting, closed the front gate, waved once more at the retreating cab, and went back into the house. It seemed empty but strangely peaceful. An inexplicable feeling of light-heartedness assailed her. Going to the piano, she dashed off a spirited rendition of *To a Wildrose* with the loud pedal down. Then she jumped up and, hum-ming, wandered out to the kitchen. The kitchen, sunny and neat, smiled at her — suddenly her own. Recklessly, she got out sugar, butter, chocolate, cream — and made a big pan of fudge, leaving the dishes piled in the sink. Then she went up-stairs and whimsically took a bath in the guest-room bathroom. Anna's presence in the house had never seemed particularly repressive; it was strange that her departure should engender such a feeling of school being out. Mr. Cugat came home and, merry and unchaperoned, they got into bathrobes, made a cocktail, and cooked crabmeat in the chafing-dish.

This holiday mood lasted just about twenty-four hours. By the end of a week Mrs. Cugat had beseechingly called three more agencies and they were taking their meals at The Corner Toasty.

It wasn't that she didn't like cooking and housework — she really loved them — but where was the time? All right, if right after breakfast you had nothing to look forward to but a long empty morning in which to plan and prepare tempting little meals, change the beds, and scour the bathroom. Fine, if right after lunch you could settle down to a brisk hour or two with the vacuum. But her life, at present, was planned so that on one day she drove a station-wagon for the Red Cross, on another she watched for planes in the interest of Civilian Defense, on another she filled out forms for the Navy, and on yet another she sewed for infant Greeks. Arriving home, late in the afternoon, from one of these various activities, to a di- shevelled, unaired house — clothes on chairs, shades awry, ashtrays full, and dishes — always dishes — piled in the sink, was very depressing. The stove began to look greasy, the pantry got full of crumbs, the bathtub acquired an ineradicable ring, and there was a grey bloom on the mirrors. She could do no more than throw open the windows and get out a dust- cloth, however, than there would be Mr. Cugat, home from the office, and hungry as a bear. The Corner Toasty seemed the practical solution, if perhaps a little limited as to menu.

It was a happy day, therefore, when, just as they had arrived at about the last DeLuxe Cheeseburger they could stomach, one of the agencies telephoned to say, briskly, that they had an experienced cook available — very high type — excellent references — only the best homes — if Mrs. Cugat would care to interview her.

Mrs. Cugat joyfully grabbed her coat and hopped into the car. At the outer door of the agency's office, however, she sud- denly encountered panic. She had never interviewed anyone before — someone else must have engaged Anna — her mother, probably. Why, for Heaven's sake, hadn't she mem- orized a little list of pertinent questions? Hands moist, she went in and advanced timidly to the desk.

'Name?' snapped the silver-haired, black crêpe receptionist with a cursory glance, pencil poised over a pad of forms. Mrs. Cugat gave it meekly.

'Any previous experience?'

'What?' said Mrs. Cugat.

'Where have you worked before?' explained the Black Crêpe distinctly, showing great patience.

'Oh, I don't want a job —' Mrs. Cugat stammered, abashed. 'I just came to interview a cook. You called me this morning. Remember?'

The Black Crêpe got very pink and glared huffily at Mrs. Cugat's bare head, polo coat, and socks. 'Pardon *me!*' she exclaimed in tones implying that so-called ladies who went around looking like part-time nursemaids deserved anything they got. 'If you'll just come this way!'

Unhappily, Mrs. Cugat followed her switching hips along a narrow aisle lined with chairs, occupied by occasional persons deep in conversation. Her upper lip had beaded with sweat. Obviously, if only to bolster her own poise, she should have dressed more sedately. An experienced cook of very high type, from only the very best homes, probably wouldn't even consider her, looking like this. At the far end of the aisle they stopped before a composed and matronly individual with pearl earrings and a sealskin coat. 'This is Mrs. Cugat, Mrs. Vanderventer,' said the Black Crêpe briefly, and switched away. Mrs. Cugat had a deranged moment during which she wasn't sure who was going to end up cooking for whom, but Mrs. Vanderventer, evidently an old hand at interviews, took things graciously in hand. Gratefully Mrs. Cugat answered her questions and strove, in spite of appearances, to give an impression of having come from one of the very best homes too. Mrs. Vanderventer's references, genteelly worded, were on crested notepaper. (They were dated 1927, but Mrs. Cugat wouldn't have dreamed of bringing it up.) Finally, after considerable deliberation, during which Mrs. Cugat looked at her hands, scarcely daring to breathe, Mrs. Vanderventer consented to come. Mrs. Cugat drove home singing.

'Darling, she sounds perfectly marvellous,' she burbled joyfully to Mr. Cugat that evening. 'So *intelligent!* Really, I don't see how we put up with Anna as long as we did!'

'Will Mrs. Vanderbilt do anything *besides* cook?' inquired Mr. Cugat, ever practical.

Mrs. Cugat hesitated. She hadn't gone into the housework end very thoroughly — or rather, Mrs. Vanderventer hadn't. 'Well,' she said optimistically, 'she's accustomed to a large staff, of course, but she says she's perfectly willing to make concessions.' Mr. Cugat looked a little sceptical at this, but only said time would tell and they departed for a farewell meal at The Toasty.

Time told. But it revealed, unfortunately, that Mrs. Vanderbilt, as she was to be forever afterward called, regarded anything in the least resembling manual labor in the light of a big concession. She occasionally dusted with the wryness of a temporarily embarrassed duchess, and once, with the air of indulging clamorous children, baked a small, dry pie. Otherwise her exertions seldom extended beyond the point of 'just opening a can of tuna,' good-naturedly scrambling a few eggs, or warming a little impromptu soup — the concession of cooking a full meal apparently being a major one and not to be expected often. Mrs. Cugat was beginning, desperately, to wonder if it wouldn't be simpler if they just gave the whole idea up and all three ate at The Toasty, when, providentially, the Vanderbilt son-in-law called one morning in a large Buick and removed her bag and baggage. He said she was needed at home. What for Mrs. Cugat couldn't imagine — unless for a fourth at bridge.

Another two weeks of The Toasty went by, and then a small town damsel by the name of Norma passed briefly through their lives. Norma never wore anything but slacks, had never cooked before, and, in less than a week, took up city ways and left to work in a parking garage.

After that, Mr. Cugat's Aunt Edith kindly sent them her own cook's deaf sister, Mildred, who was about seventy-five, broke everything she touched, but loved the place and was harder to get rid of than athlete's foot. They finally did, but Aunt Edith took it, unexpectedly, as a personal snub.

Then there was a long, bleak period during which nothing happened at all. Mrs. Cugat, just to show that she had not accepted defeat, stubbornly continued to call the employment agencies, but it was only a gesture. She gradually rearranged her life, getting the laundress to come in twice a week to clean, sending the laundry out, and resigning from plane watching. She thought once of writing appealingly to Anna, but after glimpsing her one night at The Lobster Bar, whither they had gone for respite from Cheeseburgers, she gave that up. Anna, sipping a dry martini with her friend Clara, the spot welder, was muffled in silver fox.

One Monday morning, however, when she made her routine call to the Black Crêpe at the Employment Bureau, that lady, instead of her usual laconic 'nothing yet,' said airily, 'I don't suppose, Mrs. Cugat, that *you*'d be interested in an excellent, elderly English couple? I was just about to call Mrs. Howard V. Sturm, the Third (no doubt you've heard of her), but, of course, if you'd care to interview them first —'

'Why, yes,' said Mrs. Cugat in matching tones, spurred by a variety of instincts, nearly all regrettable, 'I'll be right down.' She hung up the telephone. Evie Sturm! Having an excellent, elderly English couple simply thrust upon her! That girl had all the luck in the world — all the money, too, of course, which had something to do with it — but it was certainly maddening.

Mrs. Cugat had always aspired to a couple. In her former moments of despair over Anna's shortcomings, she used to cheer herself by picturing the happy day when, Mr. Cugat's income substantially increased, they would callously bid Anna farewell and acquire a man and wife — English, of course, and flawless like the ones in detective stories — or Evie's. The walks would always be swept, the cars shining, the brass polished, and the fires laid. No longer would all their cocktail parties take place in the pantry because Mr. Cugat was always out there making them. The telephone would be answered by a low, authoritative voice saying, 'Mr. George Cugat's residence — the name, please?' instead of Anna's harassed 'Yeah?' And when they had a dinner party, all she'd have to do would be to telephone down to the kitchen and say, 'Four extra for dinner tonight, Mrs. Hawkins — and tell Hawkins, the fruit centrepiece.'

Getting into a hat and gloves, this time, to go down to the Employment Bureau, Mrs. Cugat thought of all this wistfully — knowing full well it was a long way off. The very least an excellent English couple would ask would be three times what she could afford. Why she had ever made the appointment was beyond her, but she hadn't been able to resist it. Oh, well, maybe they would turn out to be disappointing, after all, and she would have the satisfaction of haughtily handing them back to that piece at the desk and informing her that they wouldn't do.

The couple, however, turned out to be everything anybody had ever dreamed up. They had come over with a Lady Mary Hastings, who had returned to London in a bomber, leaving them to fend for themselves, and they were modest, courteous, old-school, had accents like Noel Coward, and were named Partridge. Agonized, Mrs. Cugat implored the Black Crêpe not to call Mrs. Sturm until she had conferred with her husband and hastened over to the bank.

'Have you lost your mind?' inquired Mr. Cugat calmly, after listening to her story.

'Oh, but, darling, it's the opportunity of a lifetime — they're perfect treasures!'

'I know,' he said patiently, 'but you know, don't you, that we have just exactly half the income we had last year and twice the taxes. This is a *fine* time to decide to take on a butler!'

'I could cut down on my clothes —' she suggested eagerly.

'You're going to have to do that, anyway,' said Mr. Cugat shortly. 'Everybody is. There's a war on, you know.'

'Of course, I know!' she exclaimed. 'I'm not an idiot. But I'd like to know how the Sturms manage to sail along without cutting down on anything! Their taxes must be terrific. How do they pay them? Isn't their income cut, too?'

Mr. Cugat looked disgusted. 'The Sturms!' he exclaimed. 'Evie and Howie have been living 'way over their heads for years and everybody knows it. They're probably using their principal for taxes — they've been using it for everything else!'

'It seems to work out pretty well,' said Mrs. Cugat wistfully.

'That's what you think,' he said, with a short laugh. 'Run along now, child, I'm busy.' Forlornly, she went home and called the Employment Bureau.

The Employment Bureau was not surprised — the Black Crêpe somehow managing to imply that she'd known all along that Mrs. Cugat was just showing off. She said she had, in fact, already called Mrs. Howard V. Sturm, the Third ('no doubt you've heard of her?'), and Mrs. Sturm had said to send the Partridges right over in case Mrs. Cugat should decide that she was not willing to pay what they asked. Simmering, Mrs. Cugat hung up. Well, evidently she wouldn't have had a chance at the Partridges even if Mr. Cugat had consented — Evie paid anything — the sky was the limit. No matter what Mr. Cugat thought, it must be very simple, living on one's principal.

The telephone had no sooner left her hand, however, when it rang again. 'You cut me off so abruptly, Mrs. Cugat,' the Black Crêpe said in icy tones, 'that you gave me no opportunity to tell you that I have a very nice type colored woman here, who has just registered. Have you any objections to colored?'

'I guess not,' said Mrs. Cugat listlessly. There was a pause.

'Well, do you care to interview her?'

'No,' said Mrs. Cugat. 'Just send her over.'

'Very well,' snapped the Black Crêpe and hung up.

Mrs. Cugat sighed. A nice type colored woman — after contemplation of the Partridges! In her present mood she felt that she'd almost rather go on eating at The Toasty.

Twenty minutes later, a taxi drew up at the door. Mrs. Cugat glanced apathetically out the window. The biggest, blackest colored woman she'd ever seen in her life got out. She was dressed in a flowered print wrapper, a small mink cape, and a grey fedora. She paid the driver, waved him a gay farewell, and disappeared around the corner of the house. Tight-lipped, Mrs. Cugat went down and opened the door.

'Ma name's Vanilla,' announced this grotesque figure in dulcet tones. 'Wheyuh shell ah res' ma thin's?'

Mr. Cugat, coming in that evening, paused in the front hall, dropped his briefcase, and sniffed alertly. Rich, warm fragrances hung on the air; a cheery clatter interspersed with song came from the kitchen.

Bright-eyed, Mrs. Cugat skimmed down the stairs. 'Cross your fingers,' she implored him, 'this is too good to last, I'm afraid!'

They sat down to fried chicken, sweet potatoes, corn pone, peas in cream, and deep-dish apple pie.

'I'm afraid you're right,' said Mr. Cugat reverently. 'What have we ever done to deserve it?'

Overnight, life became again serene. Vanilla, in spite of current shortages and the intricacies of rationing, went right on producing this kind of thing. She was one of those sorceresses who can concoct a tasty entrée out of a pig's gizzard and a few beet tops, but Mrs. Cugat wondered if she wasn't getting around the butcher. She could get around almost anybody; it was her voice, which was like milk and honey.

She had a few little peculiarities, to be sure, but then, no one is perfect. One was that she never took off either the grey fedora or the mink cape even to serve dinner. ('Ah gits so cole in this climat,' she apologized), and another was that she had no last name. Also, on the day after her arrival, a small black man in a large green zoot-suit moved into a corner of the kitchen.

'Tha's Junior,' she explained him.

Junior, it appeared, had no last name either. Who he was remained a mystery — Vanilla parried inquiry deftly — but one afternoon Mrs. Cugat, visiting the third floor in search of mothballs, happened to glance into Vanilla's room as she went by and spied his hat on the dresser. She tiptoed in. His shoes were under the bed.

'Vanilla,' she said unhappily, putting her head into the kitchen, 'come to the library. I must talk to you.' Shadow darkened the sun of Vanilla's black face and she put down the egg-beater gently.

'Yessum.'

Mrs. Cugat closed the library door carefully behind them and cleared her throat. 'Vanilla,' she said, and turned a deep crimson, 'is Junior — staying here?'

Vanilla hung her head.

Mrs. Cugat examined her nails. 'Are you — married?' she asked primly.

'Well,' gulped Vanilla apologetically, 'yessum.'

Mrs. Cugat sighed in relief. 'What's the matter, can't he find work?' Vanilla was silent, her face suddenly so old that Mrs. Cugat, looking at it, felt her heart turn to butter. 'Perhaps if I tell Mr. Cugat,' she suggested consolingly, 'he'll find something for him —'

'Yessum.'

That night Vanilla surpassed even herself. But in spite of coconut cream pie, the news about Junior turned Mr. Cugat's heart to granite.

'Just a no-account lazy coon,' he declared indignantly, 'living off his wife!' Adding with horrid scepticism, 'If she *is* his wife! He certainly can *not* stay here! The sooner she's rid of him, the better!' But he did consent to write a note to somebody he thought might give Junior a job. Mrs. Cugat gave the note to Vanilla. Vanilla thanked her and Junior vanished.

A night or two later, however, home from a movie, they opened the front door and encountered a sound — a sort of rumbling, deep within the bowels of the house. Startled, they paused to listen, while it rose and fell, chuckled and died, began again. 'That damned hot-water heater!' exclaimed Mr. Cugat disgustedly after a moment. 'Remind me in the morning to send someone out to look at it.' Putting away his hat, he stretched and went toward the stairs, but Mrs. Cugat hesitated. Then she tiptoed to the kitchen, crossed to the cellar door, and opened it noiselessly. A hideous sough came out of the dark. That was no hot-water heater, that was a man trying to gargle with his throat cut! Her scalp prickled and she caught her breath, but, as she listened, she became aware of a certain familiar rhythm — a rise and fall that was, all at once, reassuring. She reached out and snapped on the light. The gargling, with a strangled snort, ceased abruptly. There was a thick, breathless silence. Peering down into the bright glare her eyes lit on Junior's hat — this time reposing on the ironing-board. Shakily, she turned out the light again and went slowly upstairs.

'Remind me about that heater,' murmured Mr. Cugat, already in bed.

'Yes,' she said thoughtfully.

She made no mention of the hot-water heater at breakfast, however, but bade Mr. Cugat farewell and went back to the dining-room to fix Vanilla with a resolute eye. Vanilla rolled two muffins off the plate she was carrying onto the floor, exclaimed, 'Lordy gub! Look whut ah done,' and disappeared under the table.

'There were some very funny noises in the cellar last night,' Mrs. Cugat went on inexorably to the broad expanse of upturned behind.

Vanilla emerged. 'Whut yo' s'pose they was?' she inquired forlornly.

'Maybe you'd better look and see.'

'Yessum.'

For the next three nights, after Mr. Cugat slept, Mrs. Cugat went down to listen at the cellar door. But all was quiet; Junior had evidently found other quarters. She had, however, an obscure feeling that he was still around. And then, one afternoon, arriving home unexpectedly, she walked into the kitchen and nearly stepped on him. He was on the floor feeding a live mouse to the cat.

'Hello, Junior,' she gasped foolishly. 'Nice to see you again!'

Junior beamed.

'Where's Vanilla?' she asked, trying to avert her eyes. Junior silently pointed, with the mouse, to the pantry door.

'Well, ah'll think it ovuh,' Vanilla's soft voice came suddenly from there — evidently into the telephone, 'but ah laks it reel well hyuh. Miz Cuga' is bein' mos' kine —' Mrs. Cugat's blood froze. Some *Judas* — actually calling right up at the house to hire Vanilla away! She wondered if it was anybody she knew. Probably.

That night, rather unexpectedly, she encountered Vanilla in the garage. Vanilla was carrying a plate of fried eggs; from the loft overhead, there came an impatient whine.

'Rats, yo' s'pose?' Vanilla ventured unhappily.

'Probably,' said Mrs. Cugat and ignored the eggs.

Junior, from there on, began to fit rather happily into the domestic scheme. He remained discreetly invisible, but there were occasional pleasant evidences of him. Mrs. Cugat went out one morning to find the car waxed, came home one afternoon to discover the garden weeded, another day the screens were put up and the porch swing hung. It was very nice — almost as good as having a couple — if you didn't object, of course, to one of them being a phantom.

Mr. Cugat, though, she knew would never put up with any such irregular arrangement as having a couple — one a phantom — however well it seemed to work out. Mr. Cugat, if she told him about Junior, would insist upon getting to the bottom of the thing, would undoubtedly send him packing, and they would, of course, lose Vanilla. Over which he would be philosophical. Mr. Cugat could be so uncompromising. He simply didn't know when he was well off; sleek and well-fed again, he had already forgotten all about cheeseburgers. So she put off telling him and decided just to go on pretending that she didn't know anything about Junior either — for a while, anyway. After all, why bring things to an unnecessary head? Mr. Cugat was in Washington a lot and tired and absorbed when he got home — they might go on comfortably like this for a long time.

Vanilla's cooking, meanwhile, seemed to grow better and better. Mrs. Cugat, having lunch one day at Evie Sturm's with The Greek Relief Sewing Circle, was elated to discover that Mrs. Partridge, late in the employ of Lady Mary Hastings, couldn't hope to touch it. Partridge himself, though, was everything anyone could ask — grave, deft, and elegant. The Sewing Circle were sickeningly impressed. 'You *lucky thing!*' they gushed. 'And to think that *marvellous* cook goes with him!' This was too much for Mrs. Cugat. It was foolhardy, she knew — all honor among friends having seemingly ceased to exist, when it came to a good cook — but she couldn't resist it; she heard herself insisting that next week the Sewing Circle come to lunch at *her* house. The Sewing Circle were delighted — particularly as next week their guiding star and patroness, the Princess Mittopoulis, was due for a visit and they had hoped to have something special to offer! They accepted with alacrity.

The Princess Mittopoulis was a little more than Mrs. Cugat had bargained for, but she had every faith in Vanilla. Vanilla was enthusiastic — she loved company. Owing to her somewhat informal appearance, however, which persisted in spite of new uniforms, Mrs. Cugat decided she'd better get Nellie Detweiler in to serve. She thought wistfully of Partridge — so nearly hers, save for a little matter of principal — and sighed. How very simple it would be to entertain, even royalty, if one had Partridge. Nellie Detweiler did all right, though. People had been getting her in to serve for as long as anybody could remember and she knew the ropes. She had only one serious fault — an aged and ailing mother, prone to sinking spells. Nellie's mother had been sinking since Mrs. Cugat's grandmother's time — her present depths defied contemplation — but Nellie said, as usual, when Mrs. Cugat called that Ma seemed a little brighter and she would be glad to oblige. Mrs. Cugat went into a happy huddle with Vanilla on the menu.

At one o'clock on the day of the luncheon, however, the living-room ahum with conversation and the Princess well into her second glass of sherry, Nellie had yet to put in an appearance. At one-fifteen, she telephoned to say that Mamma was dying. Mrs. Cugat flew to the kitchen. Vanilla, grey fedora pinned on firmly, was straining cream of watercress into cups.

'Now, now,' she crooned soothingly, when she'd heard the news, 'don' yo' fuss. Git back an' see to the cumpny wile ah considuh.'

Mrs. Cugat ran upstairs, three steps at a time, and collected one of the new uniforms and the tiny organdie cap and apron laid out for Nellie Detweiler. What this combination would look like on Vanilla hardly bore thinking about, but it was too late to figure anything else out. When she got back to the kitchen, however, Vanilla had her head in the oven tending a pan of cheese puffs and gave them only a fleeting glance. 'Ah'm 'fraid yo' soup'll git cole,' was all she said. Mrs. Cugat hurried back to the living-room to open another bottle of sherry.

The Sewing Circle were toying a bit listlessly with their glasses when she at last heard the dining-room doors open. After all, one can drink only just so much sherry. She looked up with a sigh of relief. There in the hall, in a roomy tuxedo, with a pink rose on the lapel, and a napkin over his arm, stood Junior. He flashed them a broad and gold-filled grin and announced, 'Luncheon is now bein' suhv'd in the dinin'-room!'

The Sewing Circle, after a dazzled moment, rose. Speechless, Mrs. Cugat led the way to the table. Junior swept back her chair, flipped the seat off with his napkin, and bent low. 'Mistuh Cugit's,' he hissed in her ear, pointing to the tuxedo. Mrs. Cugat waved a weak hand at the Sewing Circle. 'Sit anywhere,' she gulped, sinking down. Junior, recognizing royalty when he saw it, hastened to assist the Princess. 'Will this location be sattusfact'ry?' he inquired solicitously, choosing a pleasant sunny chair halfway down the table. The Princess accepted it graciously.

'Oh, but —' protested Mrs. Cugat, belatedly pulling herself together.

'Now,' said Junior genially, 'which of you ladies wants the Seafood Cocktail and which wants Soup?'

'Junior,' she managed, 'just bring everybody some of each,' but the order was unfortunately worded. After some delay, during which heated protestations could be heard from the pantry, he reappeared with a loaded tray of shrimp cocktail and watercress soup, professionally stacked one atop the other, and proceeded to deal them out briskly with exhortation, admonition, and encouragement. 'Jes' try this!' '*Easy* now!' 'Comin' up!'

'Where'd you find Junior?' whispered Evie Sturm, eyes alight, 'on the New York Central?'

That was it, of course! It was unmistakable — that rapid, sinuous walk — that high-balanced tray —

'Mo' buttuh, ennybuddy?' he inquired, popping out and in again with a large bowl of butter pats floating amid ice cubes. The doorbell rang, and he paused. Then, surprisingly, somewhat in the manner of a movie gangster, he tiptoed quickly over to the window, flattened his back against the wall, and peeked cautiously out over his shoulder. The bell rang again. Putting the butter down on the mantel, he vanished through the swing door.

The Sewing Circle, politely recovering themselves, sipped their soup and exclaimed in delight.

The Princess threw up her hands and rolled her eyes to heaven. But Mrs. Cugat wasn't listening. 'Perhaps I'd better go and see —' she murmured nervously as the bell continued irately and Junior failed to reappear. As she rose to her feet, the pantry door swung wide and admitted Vanilla — bearing the next course. She was, except for her face, just as Mrs. Cugat had last seen her — grey fedora, mink cape, and all — but her face was streaming with tears. All mannerly pretence on the part of the Sewing Circle was here abandoned. In wide-eyed awe, they watched Vanilla remove their plates. In spite of the undammed flow of tears and the grotesque clothes, her dignity was monumental. Whoever was at the front door started to pound. Vanilla never even raised her eyes. Four solemn-looking men suddenly passed around the side of the house, close to the dining-room windows, the last one pausing to lean forward and peer in. He then gave an exultant shout and hastened after the rest. Mrs. Cugat turned to see two policemen in the front hall. Vanilla went right on passing Eggs Encore.

'What is it? What do you want?' cried Mrs. Cugat, finally galvanized to action and hastening into the hall.

'We got a search warrant here, lady,' said a gruff voice as the hall filled with men, filing in from the kitchen. 'We got a tip this morning that there's an escaped convict from Atlanta hiding in the neighborhood. You take the attic, Clancy, and you two boys, the next floor — I'll go down to the basement with Kotecki!' They dispersed.

The Sewing Circle crowded through the dining-room door. 'The Gestapo?' breathed the Princess.

They found him on the top shelf of the linen closet. Mrs. Cugat and the Sewing Circle, noses pressed to the front windows, watched them lead him away — wistful and rumpled and still wearing Mr. Cugat's new tuxedo. Mrs. Cugat, nevertheless, felt a lump rise in her throat. He looked so little and black surrounded by all those big, ruddy Irishmen. Whatever he'd done, it seemed a shame. Poor Vanilla. She left the Sewing Circle chattering like birds and slipped off to the kitchen. Vanilla was seated at the kitchen table amid the ruins of a strawberry soufflé — her face convulsed.

'Vanilla,' crooned Mrs. Cugat consolingly, 'tell me about it!'

Vanilla turned up swimming eyes. 'Dem 'tho'ities,' she gulped, 'don' seem lak dey evuh give up! Dey come got him agin!'

'I know,' said Mrs. Cugat gently. 'But, tell me, what did Junior do?'

Vanilla wiped her eyes and fought for control. 'A long time ago,' she explained simply, 'he killed a lady.'

Mrs. Cugat opened her mouth, forgot about it, and left it that way. Finally, however, she found a word. *'Wh-why?'*

Vanilla, with the relief of sharing her grief, calmed. 'Well,' she said, wiping her eyes, 'dey ain' no nicer boy'n Junior enny-

102

wheyuh'na worl, but seems lak he tuk an instant's dislak to dis lady, firs' time he see her, an' soon it got so bad sompin' come ovuh him an' he hadda kill huh —'

'He had es-escaped fr-from Atlanta?' chattered Mrs. Cugat.

'Yessum,' said Vanilla, with some pride. 'Secun' time now. T'ain' hard. Junior's a Trusty do'n theyuh.'

Mrs. Cugat couldn't seem to think of anything to say. She blinked stupidly. Vanilla blew her nose. 'Well, t'ain' no good t'mourn, I s'pose,' she sighed philosophically, 'we'll have t'git along bes' we can —' She rose and shook out her apron, apparently done with grief. 'Mebbe it jus' as well,' she said thoughtfully, looking out the window, 'ah wuz gittin' jes a lil' worrit about him ag'in —' Mrs. Cugat's eyes widened. 'Seems lak he'd tuk an instant's dislak to Mistuh Cugit,' she explained sadly.

7

GERTRUDE

Mrs. Cugat, hands plunged into the pockets of her jacket, turned briskly into the park. Her head was up and her step, springy. It was one of those bright October mornings when the air is sharp with leaf smoke and a promise of frost, and there should be bells pealing. There were none, but she didn't mind — she felt wonderful anyway; it was just one of those days. Little yellow leaves swirled and danced on the path ahead of her and it was all she could do to keep from pirouetting and skipping in imitation. The path rounded a clump of shrubbery and climbed to a rustic bridge, arched over a small ravine, and she paused at the top to lean over and look down. At the bottom of the ravine sat a little boy sobbing, his face buried in his arms. Beside him sat a mythical-looking animal covered with grey yarn. It was attached to him by a rope. Mrs. Cugat cleared her throat, and the little boy raised his head.

'Hey,' she said, 'what are you doing down there?'

'Crying,' he replied coldly. The creature leaned over, kissed him perfunctorily on the ear and resumed quivering interest in the doings of a squirrel on the opposite bank. Fresh sobs broke forth, and, throwing his arms around the thing's neck, he buried his face in its ruff.

'Oh, here now!' protested Mrs. Cugat, hastening to the end

of the bridge, 'you mustn't cry like that!' and, with her own eyes smarting, plunged down the slippery bank.

The sobs stopped and the little boy lifted his head with a sigh, pulled a handkerchief from his back pocket, blew his nose, and turned resignedly. The beast's tail thumped politely, but its eyes stayed on the squirrel. 'Whatever is the matter?' exclaimed Mrs. Cugat, kneeling down beside them. 'Can't I do something to help?'

'No, ma'am,' said the boy with dignity, preparing to rise.

'But something must be awfully wrong to make you feel so badly,' she insisted. 'Can't you tell me? I won't tell anyone.' His tears brimmed over again and he wiped at them angrily. 'Here,' she said anxiously, pulling a bag from her pocket, 'have a peanut.'

At the sound of the crackling paper, an eager snout was thrust into Mrs. Cugat's lap. 'Down, Gertrude,' said the little boy gravely. Mrs. Cugat gave Gertrude a peanut. Gertrude kissed her gratefully.

'I don't see,' said Mrs. Cugat, getting out her handkerchief to wipe her face, 'how anybody with such a — lovely — pet could feel so sad themselves.'

'That's just it,' said the little boy.

'What?'

'My mother says I've got to get rid of her.'

'Get rid of her?'

He nodded, swallowing. 'She gets on Mr. Flambo's nerves,' he said when he could speak, adding morosely, 'Mr. Flambo's our boarder.'

'Oh, dear,' said Mrs. Cugat.

'I'm supposed to be taking her to the Animal Shelter now,' he went on, and then, suddenly opening up, 'but it just doesn't seem as if I could. The Animal Shelter is just like a jail — Gertrude won't know what to think — she's very young.'

'Couldn't you try to find another real home for her some-where?' suggested Mrs. Cugat, distressed.

'I did try — everybody in our block — but nobody'd have her.'

Gertrude, fixedly eyeing the peanuts, wagged her tail and nudged Mrs. Cugat. Mrs. Cugat gave her another and sat back on her heels. Hell! Just ten minutes ago she hadn't a care in the world — was just skipping along, glad to be alive — and now look! How could she walk out on a situation like this?

The little boy looked at her hopefully. 'You couldn't let her live at your house, I suppose,' he ventured. 'She's a very unusual-looking dog and nice to play with.'

So it was a dog. 'Oh, I hardly think so,' Mrs. Cugat inter-polated hastily.

'If you did,' he said, sighing, 'why, then, I might come over and see her once in a while.'

'But you see,' she explained, 'we have a cat.'

'Ho! That's all right,' he laughed relievedly. 'Gertrude's very nice to cats. We have one, too, and they sleep right in the same basket.'

Mrs. Cugat looked at Gertrude. She was, certainly, very unusual-looking — a little like something drawn on a cave-dweller's wall. Of course, she'd been thinking for some time that it would be nice to have a dog — but really, this one was hardly — What was she thinking of! If she had a dog, she'd want a good one — not this fantastic mongrel. 'I really think your mother's right,' she managed firmly, 'the Animal Shelter's the best thing. They're very good to them there and a dog who looks like Gertrude will probably be adopted almost at once.'

The light went out of the boy's eyes and he turned away without answering and did not look at her again. She rose determinedly and scrambled up the bank. When she reached the top, however, she made the mistake of stopping to look back.

Dishevelled and panting, she reached her own gate, tugged it open, and they bounded through, cavorted across the lawn, vaulted up the steps, and piled up at the front door. She took up more slack in the rope, got a firmer grip, and turned the knob. Gertrude, exuberance falling from her like a cloak, peered in cautiously. 'Come on,' urged Mrs. Cugat, gently tugging, 'this is your new home.' Gertrude stepped delicately over the threshold and lifted an exploring nose. Imprudently, Mrs. Cugat let go the rope and turned to hang up her coat.

'Gentul Jesus!' yelled Vanilla from the kitchen, 'whut's dis?'

Hurrying out, Mrs. Cugat found her new pet on the kitchen table, snuffing approvingly at a chocolate pie that had evidently just come from the oven, its peaks of meringue, golden. Vanilla was waving a broom.

'It's just our new dog,' panted Mrs. Cugat, staying the descending weapon as Gertrude, imperturbably, tipped the pie off onto the floor and bounded down to investigate it. 'Oh, Vanilla! I'm so sorry.'

Vanilla, the customary crescent of her lips compressed to a straight line, silently relinquished the broom, crossed to a closet, and got out a dustpan.

Indignantly, Mrs. Cugat grabbed the rope, dragged Gertrude to the back door and thrust her out. Well! She could just go home and get back on Mr. Flambo's nerves — after all, she was his problem. How had she ever got into all this?

Gertrude, with, apparently, no intention of going back to Mr. Flambo, lowered shivering haunches to the doormat and prepared to await developments. She was still sitting there alertly at six o'clock that night when Mr. Cugat came home from the office.

'What is it,' he asked blankly, 'a gnu?' Mrs. Cugat explained.

'Lord, honey,' he said, 'why didn't you tell me you wanted a dog? With the cat, I never thought you'd — I'll tell you what! The County Kennel Club are putting on a show down at the armory in a day or so and Howie says they're going to have some pretty high-class stuff. You take this thing over to the Animal Shelter in the morning and get rid of it, and then, when the Show comes, we'll go down and look them over. I've been thinking it would be nice to have a dog, too.'

Gertrude, looking from one to the other, thumped her tail enthusiastically.

'Poor thing,' said Mrs. Cugat, her conscience smiting her, 'what will we do with her tonight? We can't just leave her out here in the cold — but Vanilla is seething —'

'Oh, we'll shut her up in the garage,' he replied easily, bending to pat Gertrude's woolly poll. 'We can put a blanket or something down for her to sleep on. You'll like that, won't you, old girl?'

But Gertrude did not like it. After half an hour of outraged protest, during which the neighbors began to telephone, she came out through a window-pane and, bloody but unbowed, took up her plaint at the back door. There was nothing to do but let her in again.

'It will have to be the cellar, I guess,' said Mr. Cugat, going out in his pajamas to retrieve the blanket. But this plan proved equally impractical. Gertrude did not like the cellar either and emerged almost immediately by the simple expedient of taking the doorknob in her teeth and turning it. The cellar-door key was lost.

'Where do you suppose she *wants* to sleep?' said Mrs. Cugat despairingly. It was two o'clock and they were standing, worn and desperate, in the middle of the library — Gertrude regarding them expectantly. She had just gnawed her way half through the door from the pantry — which did have a key. Gertrude sprang into Mr. Cugat's armchair with the new slip-cover, turned around the prescribed three times, settled down with a sigh, and closed her eyes. Scarcely breathing, they tiptoed out. What she would say to Vanilla in the morning Mrs. Cugat could not imagine — and she was too tired to try.

But in the morning Gertrude was gone. She had got out, but nobody could see how. The only open windows were those on the second floor — unless, of course, she had simply unlocked a door and walked out, closing it politely behind her. She was a very unusual dog.

'Well, anyway,' Mrs. Cugat sighed relievedly, 'now I won't have to take her over to the Animal Shelter. I would have felt terribly guilty about it after promising that little boy. I don't believe I could have —'

'Well, I could have — without a qualm,' said Mr. Cugat, who had just unguardedly sat down in his armchair, and was now looking like a new cocoon. 'Poor old Flambo — there's a boy who's got my sympathy!'

'Do you think she went back there?' asked Mrs. Cugat anxiously.

'Of course. She considers that her home.'

He could not have made a more erroneous predication. At two in the morning Mrs. Cugat was roused from the depths of slumber by what she at first thought, foggily, must be a fire siren. But it was not. It was Gertrude back again.

'Let her yowl,' growled Mr. Cugat from his pillow. 'She'll get sick of it in a minute.' He was wrong again. The wails rose in length and stridency and the telephone rang.

'Are you people dead?' inquired a trenchant voice. 'Why don't you let your dog in?'

'That's not our dog, Bud,' said Mr. Cugat coolly.

'Oh, no? You were feeding it last night. What else's gonna think?'

'Okay, okay,' said Mr. Cugat hastily, as the wails switched

109

abruptly to a rataplan of shattering barks. 'Keep your shirt on—'

Gertrude bounced joyfully into the kitchen accompanied by a small fox terrier, made for the table, sniffed eagerly, and whined in disappointment.

'They're hungry, I guess,' said Mrs. Cugat blankly.

'And they're going to stay that way,' said Mr. Cugat. 'This is the last night that tramp gets me up!'

They went back to bed, leaving Gertrude still sniffing the table, the terrier, asleep in Vanilla's rocker. In the morning they were gone and in the rocker were the remains of a baked ham and part of a chocolate roll. The icebox door stood open. It seemed provident, when they let her in the next night — this time partnered by a depressed-looking spaniel — just to feed them both and raise Vanilla's wages.

'Maybe we could teach her to use a key,' Mr. Cugat said hopefully on the third night as he climbed back into bed.

'Did she bring anybody with her this time?' Mrs. Cugat asked sleepily.

'A chow.'

'I suppose she must go home every day to play with that little boy — otherwise, we'd have heard from him.' But Mr. Cugat thought not. He'd glimpsed her only yesterday, he said, in bad company behind the courthouse. 'A fine pet!' he grumbled. 'I've told the dog-catcher to be on the lookout for her.'

'I can't imagine how she gets out,' worried Mrs. Cugat. 'Do you think — a cellar window?'

'I think she's a zombie,' he said shortly.

Announcements proclaiming the opening of the County Kennel Club Show arrived. 'With Gertrude now definitely one of the family, I don't suppose there's much use going,' said Mrs. Cugat wistfully.

'Gertrude is definitely *not* one of the family,' Mr. Cugat said flatly.

'She thinks so — or she wouldn't come back every night.'

'She thinks we run a canine flop-house. I'm going to the Show tomorrow night and find you a good dog, if I have to pay a hundred and fifty dollars for it.'

Things were in full swing at the armory when they arrived and Mrs. Cugat promptly lost her heart in five or six different directions.

Liquid-eyed cockers, impudent poodles, haughty Pekinese, and a benign Saint Bernard captured her fancy in turn. But it wasn't until the dachshunds waddled into the ring that she went completely overboard. 'Oh, darling! There's the dog I've been looking for all my life!' she babbled excitedly, tugging at Mr. Cugat's sleeve. 'Look — that littlest red one all alone over on the other side of the ring. How could they take him out of line and put him 'way over there without even looking at him! He's every bit as cute as the others! Do you think he realizes and feels badly?'

Mr. Cugat did not deign to answer any of this, being interested in watching the judging. Mrs. Cugat paid no attention to it. The judges, obviously, were a set of morons. Her eyes, warm with compassion, caressed the wistful little figure and she decided she did not like its handler — an irresponsible individual in a polo coat who seemed to be giving most of his attention to his fingernails. She began to plan lovingly what she would do, when the little red puppy was hers, to make up for the neglect and humiliation it was suffering.

Therefore, it came as quite a surprise when it was awarded the blue ribbon. She was delirious with surprise. 'But they never even looked at him!' she gabbled, 'and they spent hours over the others!'

'They were picking Second and Third,' explained Mr.

Cugat — 'that little bitch that got First is a three-time champion.'

'George, how can you!'

'What?'

'Call that darling little thing a bitch!'

'Because, sweet, it *is* one.'

'Oh.'

'The Sturms have a box somewhere, shall we go find them?' he asked, smiling and squeezing her arm.

'Not until I find where they keep him — her, I mean. I want to see it close up.'

'Run along, then, I'll be with the gang.'

Mrs. Cugat skipped joyfully off. She found her darling at the end of a long row, in a stall that looked like the royal box at the opera. It was upholstered with ribbons — predominantly blue — and flanked with silverware. It was also roped off. Mrs. Cugat scrambled eagerly under the rope. The little red creature wriggled with pleasure and thumped its tail.

'Don't handle her, please!' said a cool voice. Mrs. Cugat turned, abashed. The speaker was a woman, probably no older than herself, but of a type that, somehow, always made her feel about twelve years old. Tall, small sleek head, tweeds, and big square sapphires. 'She doesn't care for cooing,' observed this individual in a drawling voice and turned to speak to the handler. 'Not a bad little show, at that, Quinby.' Mrs. Cugat turned to give the dachshund a last pat. '*Didn't you hear me?*' The tones were silver, but each word dropped separately. Mrs. Cugat scrambled out from under the rope.

'She's so darling — I couldn't resist,' she apologized. The woman, looking right through her, went on talking to Quinby. Mrs. Cugat's face reddened. Well, really. Who in the world did Smoothie, here, think she was? Dog-show people! Mrs. Cugat delicately dusted her hands and tucked a stray curl back into place. 'As a matter of fact,' she said with the rather cultured accent she'd picked up at school, but hadn't used very lately, 'I was thinking of buying her.'

The woman turned. 'Oh, yes?' she said. Aha! thought Mrs. Cugat, you're singing a different tune now, aren't you?

'Yes. My husband is probably willing to pay as high as a hundred and fifty for her,' she said offhandedly.

The handler laughed shortly. The woman, pushing Mrs. Cugat's shoulder gently out of her way, sauntered off. Mrs. Cugat glared after her.

'Sister,' said the handler, 'the Carringtons were offered four hundred for that bitch last week.'

'Dollars?' stammered Mrs. Cugat. He looked at her pityingly.

She returned to Mr. Cugat, in the Sturms' box, decidedly subdued. The Sturms were off somewhere, but there were some other people there, watching a class of springers. Mrs. Cugat settled down to lick her wounds — an indulgence, however, that was to be short-lived. The Sturms reappeared and, with them, to her horror, the sapphire woman. 'My dear, you know who it is, don't you?' Evie rattled like a muffled machine gun in her ear while Howie began introductions. 'Pamela Carrington — they've moved here from Philadelphia — he was a M.F.H. — but he's terribly patriotic and has taken a job, vice-president or something of Acme Aircraft — theirs is that divine Daimler we've been seeing around town. And *what* jewelry! They've rented the Buchard place.' Mrs. Cugat had just time to sniff and say 'Really?' before it was her turn. Amusement flicked momentarily in Mrs. Carrington's eyes as recognition dawned, but she said nothing and acknowledged the introduction graciously.

'And Mr. Cugat —'

'Hello, George.'

113

'Hello, Pam! So you finally got here,' exclaimed Mr. Cugat warmly. 'The Carringtons were very nice to me down in Washington,' he explained, and Mrs. Carrington proceeded to take up right where she'd left off. The rest began waxing cosmopolitan. Remarks like 'Tommy, wasn't it in Cannes that we ran into the Whitneys,' and 'I'll never forget one time at Aiken,' were carted in and laboriously dumped — everybody getting the familiar best foot out in front — except Mrs. Cugat, who spent the rest of the evening with her feet wrapped around the rungs of her chair and her chin on her chest.

'You never told *me* anything about meeting the Carringtons in Washington,' she sniffed when they got home.

'Didn't I?' said Mr. Cugat offhandedly. 'One of those things. Just slipped my mind, I guess.'

'You never tell me anything about the people you meet and the fun you have in Washington.'

'Fun!' he squawked. 'Just you try it once!'

'Well, you seem to have been pretty pally with the beautiful Pamela —'

'She's a nice kid,' said Mr. Cugat.

'You can have her.'

'Ha! You aren't jealous?' he chortled, pleased.

'Certainly not, I just think she's affected.'

'I know what you mean — but you'll like her better when you get to know her. You'd better go call or something. They went out of their way to be nice to me.'

Mrs. Cugat said nothing — but calling on Pamela Carrington was one of those things that was just going to slip *her* mind. She went to sleep and dreamt that Mrs. Carrington's little dachshund was crying in the dark. She awoke, of course, to find it was only Gertrude — wanting in and bringing a collie.

The next few days were filled with parties in honor of the Carringtons. People put away their rum and got out their Scotch, long dresses and lace tablecloths — paced, for the most part, by Evie Sturm, who liked nothing better than to make the rich and famous happy. 'She's even had the swimming pool filled again,' said Mrs. Cugat disgustedly. 'She had it emptied for the duration because she heard the Rockefellers did.' Everybody, it seemed, went to call. It began to look as if Mrs. Cugat would have to. Mr. Cugat was beginning to be puzzled by her putting it off and she simply couldn't tell him about the dog show — he might be ashamed of her. And so, lips grimly set, she borrowed her mother's sable scarf one afternoon and set out.

The 'Buchard place' had been a hideous, sprawling, Hollywood Spanish house in the wrong part of town, but Mrs. Cugat had to admit, as she turned into the driveway, that the Carringtons had done wonders with it. The curly iron fence had been replaced by pickets, the orange stucco walls demurely whitewashed, and cascades of late petunias blossomed between lavender shutters. She got out of the car and walked glumly up the gravel path. Her pessimism, however, was lifted almost immediately by having the door opened by no other than Evie Sturm's butler, Partridge, who had the grace to look almost uncomfortable.

'Why, hello, Partridge,' she said, brightening, 'what have you done — made a change?'

'Well, yes, madam,' he admitted.

'Mrs. Partridge, too?' she said, stepping into a white hall filled with roses.

'Oh, yes, madam.'

'Well, well. I'm glad it's someone we know. Mrs. Partridge's cooking is something I should miss.'

'Thank you, madam, I'll tell her,' he said, and slithered off.

Pamela Carrington came into the room with a quick, light step. 'My dear,' she said, 'how sweet of you to come!' She had on a pale blue gingham pinafore, bare brown legs, and a

king's ransom in rubies. Which, for some reason, seemed to
look all right — probably because the pinafore cost as much as
the rubies.

Mrs. Cugat, reduced again to a fuzzy-haired schoolgirl,
said she thought the house was 'just darling.' Pamela shrugged
and said it was impossible, of course, but — Fun. A real
Challenge. 'Pepe's so terribly serious about this war business,
you know,' she smiled, 'he insisted we live near the plant so
he'd be just one of the men. I thought to myself, when I
heard we were coming here, I can't *bear* it! No shops, no
theatres, no museums! But, do you know — I *adore* it! Everyone's so simple and friendly. And, after all, it's only tem-
porary. Would you like to see the rest?'

'Oh, yes,' said Mrs. Cugat.

'This is the dining-room,' Pamela said, leading the way.
'Dinky, of course, but it didn't come out too badly.' The
dining-room had a small fountain, a mirror in the ceiling, and
a marble floor flanked by six well-grown bay trees.

'It's just darling,' said Mrs. Cugat. What was the *matter*
with her? Didn't she know any other words? They went out
to look at the garden. Squads of men were everywhere —
digging up shrubbery here, putting it in there. At the back
of the garage were two long wire enclosures, floored with new
concrete, and in one lay the little red dachshund, dozing in the
sun. Without being able to help it, Mrs. Cugat fell to her
knees and cooed.

'That's Baby Brunhilda of Mecklinburg — you've probably
heard of her,' said Pamela lightly.

'Of course,' said Mrs. Cugat. 'She's just darling!'

'I'm so thrilled,' Pamela went on, really looking thrilled;
'we've had her bred to Dortmund's Champion Bismarck
Schönhausen — we really ought to get something perfect in
the way of puppies!'

'Dachshunds are such shiny little things,' said Mrs. Cugat

wistfully, thinking of Gertrude's matted grey wool; 'I'd rather have one than anything I know of.'

'You would? Would you like a puppy?' asked Pamela politely.

'Oh! I didn't mean it *that* way,' protested Mrs. Cugat, reddening. 'You're terribly nice, but we couldn't possibly — we already have a *lovely* dog!'

'Really? Well, let me know if you change your mind. Baby B's are usually something rather special — she never has more than four, but I know Pepe would like to give you one.' They retired to the house, Mrs. Cugat protesting feebly. Partridge was bringing in the tea things — among them a plate of familiar-looking sandwiches — most of Evie's rarities. 'Oh, very nice,' said Pamela smiling upon him. Mrs. Cugat began to relax a little. Pamela really could be very gracious.

'This china is just darling,' she said, and bit at her tongue savagely. There was a long low wail at the front door.

'God! What's that?' exclaimed the hostess, nearly dropping the teapot. Mrs. Cugat listened, frozen, as it rose again. Pamela put down the pot, ran to the window, and looked out. Her jaw dropped. 'Come, look!' she cried. 'Something's escaped from the zoo!'

But Mrs. Cugat didn't have to look — there was no mistaking that wail. Tight-lipped, she went to the window. Pamela was now laughing — long silvery peals that brought tears to her eyes.

'It's just my dog,' said Mrs. Cugat, very red.

'Oh, my dear! I'm so sorry — but really! It looks like something someone might have — knitted!'

Mrs. Cugat looked out. Gertrude, her petticoats matted with filth, squatted before the door, her head raised in invocation. A sudden fierce loyalty to her welled up within Mrs. Cugat. After all, just because Pamela had never happened to have seen a dog that looked like Gertrude, there was no reason to go off into gales of rude laughter. It was very impolite. Baby Brunhilda, herself, would look pretty funny if you'd never seen a dachshund.

'What on earth *is* it?' Pamela was gasping.

'Indian Coach Dog,' Mrs. Cugat said coldly, 'from Dakar. A friend of George's — a maharaja (easy now!) sent her to us.'

Pamela stopped laughing and looked at her sharply.

'Really?' she said. 'I've never heard of the breed.'

'I don't suppose you have,' said Mrs. Cugat shortly. 'They're very rare. She's the only one in the country.' (One could be sure of that!)

Pamela wiped her eyes and looked out the window again.

'Amazing,' she murmured. 'Do you suppose she's correctly plucked?'

'What?' said Mrs. Cugat.

'Plucked correctly,' explained Pamela. 'Those long trailing skirts give her such an extraordinary shape —'

'I don't know,' said Mrs. Cugat shortly. 'That's the way she was when we got her.' Gertrude here turned, caught sight of Mrs. Cugat in the window, and began yelping with delight and showing every sign of coming right through the glass. 'Oh, dear,' Mrs. Cugat said nervously, 'I'm afraid I'll have to go without my tea. She'll come right through the window if I leave her out there and we can't let her in with all that dirt on her —'

Pamela rang for Partridge. 'Take Mrs. Cugat's er — dog — back and shut her up in that empty run until she's ready to leave,' she said, and added, turning to Mrs. Cugat, 'She'll go with him, I suppose?'

'Oh, yes,' said Mrs. Cugat uneasily.

No good could come of this. Partridge, a moment later, romped past the window, coat tails flying.

'When was George in India?' inquired Pamela interestedly.

'A long time ago,' said Mrs. Cugat and changed the subject.

When they went out to get Gertrude, they found, as usual, that she had defied incarceration and had escaped from the run. She was in Baby B's run — finishing off her dinner.

Baby Brunhilda's impending accouchement, like everything to do with the Carringtons, caused quite a ripple in the social stream. The bridge club was ahum with it.

'Have you *heard* the latest? The Carringtons are importing a special vet all the way from Baltimore! I ask you!'

'They're frantic. Baby B won't eat anything but sardines.'

'They say you have to pay a perfectly terrific stud fee to get Dortmund's What-his-name —'

'Oh, my dear, you do! But Pepe expects to get a hundred and fifty apiece for the puppies.'

'Howie's buying me one,' said Mrs. Sturm smugly.

'Pepe's giving me one,' said Mrs. Cugat, retiring Mrs. Sturm.

She went home to find the lights on in the library and Mr. Cugat already there. 'Hello?' she said brightly, sticking her head in the door. He was kneeling in front of the fire. On the hearth sat Gertrude, stiffly, head averted, eyes half-closed, a rope around her neck. Beside her sat a basketful of squeaking, struggling little woolly grey mice. Mrs. Cugat stared, her mouth open. 'My gosh,' she breathed finally, 'what are those? G-G-Gertrude hasn't had — puppies?'

Mr. Cugat looked up with a grin. 'In a manner of speaking — yes,' he said. Then, as she continued to stare stupidly, explained, 'Pamela Carrington sent them over this afternoon with her compliments and says to tell you that Baby Brunhilda is doing as well as can be expected.'

'*Baby Brunhilda!*' gasped Mrs. Cugat dazedly. 'Do you mean — *these* are Baby B's new puppies?'

'So it would seem,' said Mr. Cugat.

'But they can't be!' protested Mrs. Cugat, dropping to her knees beside the basket. 'There're so many — and they look just like Gertrude!'

'They certainly do,' agreed Mr. Cugat, adding gently, 'Pamela also sent over what I find is a pretty practical suggestion —'

'What?'

'She thinks we'd better change her name to Gus.'

8

IN THE TEMPLE OF MAMMON

Mrs. Cugat skipped across the bronze threshold of the Tri-State Trust with a bright nod for its braided doorman and proceeded across the terrazzo to the customers' desks. She had to write a counter check to Cash, there being a sale in progress at the Bib and Tucker Shoppe — which carried on its thriving little business under an inflexible aegis labelled 'No Credit.' She chose a pen and craned her neck to get a glimpse of Mr. Cugat, who sat over behind a low mahogany fence on which rested his name in a small gold picture frame. Mr. Cugat was not looking her way; he was examining some papers and listening with an intent expression to the words of an impressive individual who sat across the inkwells from him. Mrs. Cugat disappointedly lowered her eyes and went about the business at hand. Her pen hesitated momentarily when she came to write in the amount; besides ten dollars for the Bib and Tucker, she needed three dollars for Mr. Fisher who would be through, tonight, cleaning up the yard, six dollars for that woman who was doing the hall curtains, a dollar for a manicure, a dollar, say, for lunch, and five dollars and sixty-three cents for the gas bill which she had forgotten again until today, the last day of the discount. Mr. Cugat became somewhat irate if she lost the gas company's discount too often. Over a period of five years, he was wont to say — with no visible effort at figuring — she could save approximately nineteen dollars and begged her to think of all the things she could do with nineteen dollars. Yes — well. The Yard, The Curtains, Manicure, Lunch, Gas Bill, Sale — she

121

figured carefully on the Tri-State's immaculate blotter — twenty-six dollars and sixty-three cents. Quite a lot. Maybe she'd better just get ten dollars now and come back and get the rest later. It was not sensible to go into a place like the Bib and Tucker with twenty-six dollars and sixty-three cents in your purse, certainly. Prudently, and pleasantly conscious of it, she wrote Ten and no/100. She'd get one little hat — maybe a scarf. That was all.

Folding two polleny new fives into her bag, she left Mr. Facey's window and went through the swinging gate in Mr. Cugat's fence, to see if there was a chance of him taking her to lunch. The impressive gentleman was still there, sitting forward in his chair and waving a well-manicured hand, adorned with a twinkling diamond, to accent his pronouncements. The desk was strewn with documents and his face looked stern and admonitory as he pointed to them.

'I'm warning you,' he said, as Mrs. Cugat hovered diffidently in the background, 'things look pretty serious and if you don't act soon, you're in for trouble!' Adelaide, Mr. Cugat's secretary, tiptoed up, laid some papers gently before him, gave the gentleman a cold look, Mr. Cugat a compassionate smile, and shunted Mrs. Cugat to an outlying chair. Adelaide, known to most of Mr. Cugat's envious associates as 'Miss America,' rankled, somewhat, in Mrs. Cugat's breast; she had even lowered herself once or twice to protest that there wasn't a woman of her acquaintance who would stand for their husband's secretary looking like that, but Mr. Cugat had not deigned to answer. 'Thanks, Lottie,' he said now, without looking up, shifted uneasily in his chair, bit a nail, and bent absorbedly over another paper.

Lottie! thought Mrs. Cugat.

'They'll get the best of you,' the gentleman averred grimly, wrenching his eyes from the departing Adelaide, 'and then there'll be nothing left for you to do but *close up!*'

'We can't do that!' Mr. Cugat protested.

'There'll be no alternative,' said the gentleman and threw up his hands.

Mrs. Cugat stared at his back in alarm. Close up? The Bank! Like before? A medley of distressing pictures obliterated disapproval. 1932. Coming home from school to find her mother's house bereft of all servants save old Caroline. The music-room shut off to save heat. The town car jacked up. Aunt Florence Hathaway selling cold cream, Melba DeKoven selling *Harper's Bazaar*, everybody cutting down to one movie a week and washing her own hair and playing bridge for a twentieth.

'Good morning, Mary Elizabeth,' a voice said tersely, and Mr. J. Duncan Atterbury, august president of the Tri-State Trust, trundled by on the other side of the fence and turned in at Mr. Cugat's gate.

'Oh, good morning!' whispered Mrs. Cugat, pursuing him with anxious eyes.

'Good morning, sir,' said Mr. Cugat sombrely. 'Here's Mr. Honeywell from the Paragon people — he says things are pretty bad. We may have to close.'

'Impossible!' barked Mr. Atterbury, outrage in his tone; 'we can't do that!'

'Mr. Honeywell says there may be no alternative,' said Mr. Cugat gloomily, and ran his fingers distractedly through his hair.

'Funny you people didn't wake up to the situation sooner,' marvelled Mr. Honeywell, with a pitying shake of his head.

'My dear sir,' expostulated Mr. Atterbury coldly, 'one never expected that an institution of this sort —' He stopped, obviously moved and sighed. 'I'll put the whole thing in your hands, George. It's up to you. Do whatever's necessary — the personnel will co-operate,' and, turning on his heel, he walked off with his head bent.

'The situation and its consequences are graver than you

realize,' said Mr. Honeywell darkly. Mrs. Cugat stared at him hostilely. Was that so! Well, they'd come through it before, they could do it again. Vanilla would have to go, of course, and the cars probably sold. The yard-man would have to be dispensed with — but Mr. Cugat could mow the lawn. They would undoubtedly resign from the golf club and close up part of the house so that it would be easier to take care of. If she'd only bought that expensive tweed suit and top-coat last week — then, at least, she would have had something to see her through. She reviewed her last winter's clothes glumly. Perfect rags — all of them.

'I advise you to come to an immediate decision,' said Mr. Honeywell, rising. 'We'll be waiting to hear.'

Immediate! The bank, in that case, might very well be closed by tonight. And she had only ten dollars in her purse. But, she thought suddenly, there was three hundred dollars in her account. She rose hurriedly from her chair and made for the customers' desks. It was most unethical for a bank official to withdraw his money from a tottering bank in the nick of time — Mr. Cugat, of course, would never — but she was not a bank official and Mr. Cugat did not know. She would take the money home and put it away for emergencies. They might need it in case of serious illness or accident. Or perhaps Mr. Cugat might require just that much for some new business venture. How proud she'd be to be able, due to her own canny foresight, to produce it for him. Nervously, she wrote the check and went over to Mr. Facey's window. Mr. Facey, all unaware of the walls crumbling about him, smiled cheerfully. With trembling fingers she pushed the check through. Would he suspect anything? It would never do to have him start wondering about it later.

Mr. Facey scanned the check briefly and opened his drawer. 'How do you want it?' he asked pleasantly. 'In fifties? Or something smaller?'

'Oh, fifties will be — *fine!*' Mrs. Cugat gulped and Mr. Facey counted out six. She gathered them up and put them in her bag.

'Darling!' she breathed, back at Mr. Cugat's desk, her cheeks pink. 'What is it? I couldn't help hearing! What can I do to help?'

'What do you know about ants?' inquired Mr. Cugat glumly.

'Ants?'

'Yes,' he said, 'we have ants.'

'*Ants?*'

'I said ants,' said Mr. Cugat. 'We have ants.'

'You mean,' she ventured after a little, 'that the bank — has ants?'

'That's right,' he sighed, 'like this —' and he opened a folder to reveal a huge and intricate insect with wily eyes and glossy bulges, horridly depicted in full color.

Mrs. Cugat recoiled. '*Where?*' she squeaked.

'Everywhere — that one's highly magnified, dear — offices, vaults, cages, boardroom — we're crawling. And it's the darndest thing, no one can figure out how we got them. That was the exterminator who just left and he says in Paragon's forty years' experience, this is the first time they ever had a bank with ants.'

'George, how awful!'

'Terribly embarrassing for us,' said Mr. Cugat. 'Undignified.'

Mrs. Cugat held her feet up off the floor. 'What are you going to *do?*'

'We hardly know yet,' he said, and leaned his forehead wearily on his hand. 'The essential thing, this fellow says, is to get the queen.' He handed Mrs. Cugat a second folder showing an even more elaborate creature, intimately absorbed in unfolding a wing. 'This is her,' he explained, 'getting ready to go on her nuptial flight.'

Mrs. Cugat looked and swallowed. 'Is she coming back?' she faltered.

'She is back,' he replied grimly, 'and laying eggs. But that's just it — we don't know where. We're going to have to sprinkle stuff around.'

'In the *bank?*' she gasped, shocked. Subject this gleaming Carrara and silky bronze to the homely nostrums of a dirty pantry?

'There's a slow-working poison we can use,' said Mr. Cugat, adding wryly — 'may catch one or two of that nosey bunch over in the trust department, of course —'

'You'll be careful, won't you?' she put in anxiously.

Mr. Cugat ignored this. 'The worker ant,' he said, in pedagogical tones, 'has to try the stuff first. If he likes it, he takes some home to his queen. But you have to be careful that it's not too strong or it kills him before he gets there. On the other hand, if it's not strong enough, it won't kill her — she's pretty tough. And, of course,' he added, 'there may be two queens — a sweet ant queen and a grease ant queen. In that case there'll be months of experiment.'

'How will you ever know?'

'I can't imagine,' he said disconsolately.

'Well, I should think,' Mrs. Cugat said indignantly, 'that there'd be some quicker and more scientific way of getting rid of just ants in this day and age. I'll bet those Paragon people tried this on the Ark.'

'Oh, there's a modern way,' said Mr. Cugat soberly, 'only we can't use it.'

'Why?'

'Because you have to shut the whole place up for four or five days and use gas.'

'Can't we do that?'

'Certainly not!' he exploded. 'You're as bad as Honeywell. Nobody ever seems to realize that you can't just close a bank whenever you want a little time out like you would to re-decorate a night club or something. I guess people'd realize pretty quick, though, if they found signs plastered all over the front of the place some morning. Beware! Poison Gas! Do not Enter! Paragon's Pest Paralyzer. And you can imagine,' he added, reddening, 'the laugh they'd get over at the Corn Exchange!'

Mrs. Cugat, however, was suddenly no longer listening. So *that's* all they meant by having to close the bank! She sagged in her chair with relief. No need for heroic sacrifice, after all. The cars, good old Vanilla, Mr. Fisher, the golf club were safe. She could buy some new clothes — that tweed suit, for instance. She'd better get it right away. Look how nearly she came to being caught with literally nothing to put on her back. She gazed gratefully around the Tri-State's lofty lobby. What were a few ants! Mr. Cugat still had his fortune, his honor, his integrity —

'Oh, what are a few ants!' she exclaimed gaily.

Mr. Cugat muttered and buried himself in another folder — one showing an unwary worker ant emerging with a pleased, replete look from a doorway labelled Paragon's Pest Paste. He said hurriedly that — no, he couldn't take her to lunch to celebrate — celebrate what? — he was going to poke around back in the Loan Department and see, if maybe, they hadn't left a cake or something lying around. The Loan Department were always having some damned party or other — one of them had a birthday back there every other day.

Mrs. Cugat, buoyant with the rapture of restored wealth, rose, humming lightly, and dropped a comforting pat on his hunched shoulder. 'Flour and black pepper is good, I've heard,' she offered kindly, and still humming left him and spun blithely out through the whirling blades of the Tri-State's proud but guilty door to make off up the street for the Bib and Tucker.

9

FALSE WITNESS

HEH, HEH, HEH,' chuckled Mr. Cugat with a reminiscent look in his eye, as he slowly stirred his breakfast coffee. Mrs. Cugat raised her brows in polite inquiry. 'I had the damnedest dream last night,' he elucidated.

Mrs. Cugat went back into her newspaper. There is, perhaps, nothing in the world so peculiarly devoid of interest as somebody else's dreams — and Mr. Cugat seemed to have been dreaming an awful lot lately. Overwork, she supposed. Like all dreamers, of course, he had to tell you.

Mr. Cugat's dreams were, generally, of the marvellous variety, involving him in complicated situations like being atop a roof, surrounded by frogs and unable to climb to the ridgepole without stepping on some of them. The details, meticulously related, usually went right into one of Mrs. Cugat's ears and out the other without intruding, in any way, on what she was thinking. But this morning, right in the middle of *Terry and the Pirates*, she suddenly heard him say, 'And there I was, chasing across the tenth green in my bathing suit after Laura Maxwell — of all people!'

'Laura Maxwell!' exclaimed Mrs. Cugat, lowering her paper.

'She had on a bathing-suit, too,' went on Mr. Cugat innocently. 'Green — one-piece.'

'And did you catch up with her?' inquired Mrs. Cugat.

128

Mr. Cugat appeared to think. Then he slapped his knee and wagged his head.

'Aren't dreams amazing,' he chortled. 'Do you know what I was trying to catch her for?' Mrs. Cugat was silent. 'She had a picture of a fish tattooed on her leg,' he exploded, weak with merriment, 'and I wanted to ask her why. After that,' he went on slowly, frowning in an effort at recollection, 'we seemed to come to a sort of lake and she said she'd like me to teach her to swim!'

Mrs. Cugat put down her napkin. 'Well,' she said, 'this is interesting. How long has it been going on?'

Mr. Cugat looked up, startled. 'What?' he asked.

'You and Mrs. Maxwell — Laura, to you.'

Mr. Cugat put down his spoon. 'Honey,' he said gently, leaning toward her over his plate, his eyes calm, 'this was in a *dream*.'

'It would have to be,' she retorted caustically; 'nowhere else would a cow like that ever dare come out in a "one-piece" bathing-suit!'

Mr. Cugat picked up his spoon again. 'She looked pretty darned good in it, as a matter of fact,' he said dryly, and dipped into his egg. Mrs. Cugat dipped into hers.

'How long have we been calling her Laura?' she inquired lightly.

Down went Mr. Cugat's spoon again. 'For Pete's sake,' he said softly, 'what is all this? I don't call her Laura. I don't even know her — except in a business way. She carries an account at the bank. Her husband's a marine or something. She's called me up a couple of times about his checks coming through, and since we met her that time at the Delanceys' cocktail party, she naturally always says, "This is Laura Maxwell speaking."' He lifted his coffee cup, drained off its contents, threw down his napkin, and came around the table to kiss her good-bye. But Mrs. Cugat, without being able to help it, turned her head away and so, after standing motionless a moment, he turned on his heel and went out — slamming the door.

She was instantly ashamed. What in Heaven's name had possessed her? What ridiculous tricks one's more primitive instincts could play! She had been, momentarily, just as jealous as if Mr. Cugat really had been chasing Mrs. Maxwell across the tenth green to find out about her tattoo. He'd dreamt he had, though — and enjoyed it thoroughly, by the light in his eye, she thought resentfully. Men!

Mrs. Maxwell was a newcomer in town. She was, so the story went, living with an aunt — whom nobody seemed to know — while her husband was in the service. She spent a good deal of time at the Country Club playing golf with the pro and was statuesque, blond, aloof, and given to snoods.

Mrs. Cugat, however, by dinner-time, had evidently forgotten all about her and the atmosphere of the evening meal was one of normal symphony. But two days later, Mrs. Maxwell strolled past the front porch of the Country Club and came abruptly back into their lives.

Mr. and Mrs. Cugat and the Sturms and the Blakes and Cory Cartwright, home on leave, and one or two other people were sitting there in a row, tilted back in their chairs, their feet propped up, having a leisurely drink. It was Sunday afternoon and they'd just finished golf.

'I wonder who that woman ever sees,' remarked Mrs. Blake idly, as Mrs. Maxwell, tall, self-contained, and alone, stepped up to tee off. 'Doesn't anybody know her?'

'George does,' said Mrs. Cugat demurely.

Everybody turned to look at Mr. Cugat, who reddened perceptibly.

'Liz — for Pete's sake!' he protested.

'Do you, George? How come?' inquired Evie Sturm, interested.

'She banks with us,' muttered Mr. Cugat. 'That's all I know about her.'

'Why, George!' expostulated Mrs. Cugat. 'He's so shy,' she crooned. 'Tell Evie, darling, all about you and Mrs. Maxwell running around in your bathing-suits — out on the tenth green. She wants George to teach her to swim,' she explained. This created quite a stir. Mr. Cugat glared and Mrs. Cugat tipped happily back and forth in her chair. 'He says,' she went on impishly, 'that she wears a green bathing-suit — one piece — and looks simply gorgeous in it.'

'I'll bet she does, at that,' said Cory speculatively, and the eyes of every man in the row sought the unconscious figure of Mrs. Maxwell languidly picking up her tee, and lingered there appraisingly.

'She has one particularly fascinating feature,' went on Mrs. Cugat, goaded by she knew not what, 'George says she has a picture of a fish tattooed on her hip.'

'Her knee,' growled Mr. Cugat.

'A picture of a *fish?*' breathed Mrs. Sturm.

'George, old son, what have you been up to since I've been gone?' murmured Cory, awed.

Mrs. Cugat here caught an exchange of wide-eyed glances behind her back and decided it was about time to end her little joke. There was a blood-curdling scream from the direction of the pool followed by a splash. Everybody stood up.

'Sounds like somebody fell in!' exclaimed Mr. Cugat.

It was, it turned out, none other than the Sturms' little Letty Lou, who had been pushed in by the Blakes' little Butch. In the ensuing umbrage Mrs. Cugat's provocative revelations anent Mr. Cugat's unsuspected carryings-on were completely forgotten — but not, it appeared, for long.

On the following Tuesday evening, when she and Mr. Cugat walked into the Sturms' living-room for their customary weekly bridge game, she was somewhat taken aback to discover, sitting on the couch, dressed in trailing green pajamas and a gilt snood — none other than the suddenly ubiquitous Mrs. Maxwell. Mrs. Cugat threw Mr. Cugat a startled, involuntary glance. His face was a mask. Then she saw Cory's khaki-clad figure coming through the door, bearing a tray of drinks. Of course! A very nice idea of Evie's. Nobody loved a new feminine face like Cory and on his first leave they were doing their utmost to please and pamper him. Mrs. Sturm, however, following with a bowl of ice cubes, crippled this optimistic theory right from the start.

'Liz, you and Cory and Howie and I'll play bridge here and Laura and George can play gin rummy over at that table by the fire,' she said briskly, throwing Mr. Cugat an arch and obvious glance. Mr. Cugat did not demur. Cory pulled out Mrs. Cugat's chair with a flourish.

Mrs. Cugat's bridge was not good. That devil, Evie! Just suppose Mr. Cugat really was chasing after Mrs. Maxwell — and for all Evie knew, he was — there had been, as yet, no opportunity to explain that idiotic dream. A fine friend she was — deliberately promoting the affair. That dream business was going to be a little difficult to bring up again, too. One cannot say, out of a clear sky, 'Look here, George doesn't really chase Mrs. Maxwell around, he just dreams he does.' It sounded almost worse. One could not say it tonight, certainly, with Mrs. Maxwell sitting right there. There was no telling what interpretation she might put on it. Probably think Mr. Cugat was crazy about her and be pleased as punch. Mrs. Cugat gave them a covert glance. The woman was good-looking, no getting around it — in a big, spear-bearing way. They were playing decorously. Mrs. Maxwell didn't seem to have much to say. In fact, unless one asked her a direct question she never said anything at all, come to think of it. Just smiled.

'Well, did you and your Laura have a nice cosy time?' she asked tartly on the way home. Mr. Cugat turned to look at her impassively. 'She plays a nice game,' he said carelessly. Rebuffed, Mrs. Cugat subsided. Mr. Cugat began to whistle cheerily, 'Avalon.' He always whistled 'Avalon' when he was feeling particularly pleased with life.

Thursday was Harrison Blake's birthday party. 'Darling,' sang Mrs. Blake to Mrs. Cugat over the telephone in the morning, 'I've asked George's Mrs. Maxwell tonight — I simply had to — everybody's intrigued — so will you bring her?'

Mrs. Cugat started to protest that Mrs. Maxwell was not George's and then thought better of it. 'Okay,' she said laconically, 'where's she live?'

'Why, I don't know,' said Mrs. Blake, nonplussed, and then added uncollectedly, 'but George must, doesn't he? — I mean —'

'I'll ask him,' said Mrs. Cugat crisply; 'we'd love to bring her, of course.'

'We've been asked to call for "your" Mrs. Maxwell,' she announced shortly, that evening, climbing into the car beside Mr. Cugat.

Mr. Cugat grinned. 'Where's she live?' he asked.

'*I* don't know. Don't you?'

'Nope.'

'George, will you stop looking like a male Mona Lisa! You're being perfectly insufferable. I know all this is my fault, but you needn't rub it in. Here you are, all due to me, suddenly transformed into a wolf and loving it — while I sit around and watch people feel sorry for me. It does seem the very least you could do is to be a little sympathetic too.' Mr. Cugat started whistling 'Avalon.' 'Where are you going?' she asked sharply, as they turned out of the driveway.

'Over to the Club to find out my dream-girl's address,' said Mr. Cugat blithely.

133

Mr. Cugat was asked to take Mrs. Maxwell in to dinner —
Mrs. Maxwell, really lovely tonight in gold-colored crêpe
with a black chenille snood, as smiling and impassive as ever.
During cocktails the men had literally flocked around her and
Mrs. Cugat noted wrathfully quite a little air of proprietary
pride apparent in Mr. Cugat's manner. Maddeningly,
though, he did absolutely nothing that you could put your
finger on and upbraid him for — unlike Howie Sturm and
one or two others who, as the evening wore on, grew positively
fatuous — he just looked smug. Mrs. Cugat could have wrung
his neck.

Driving home after the party she tried to keep up an uncon-
cerned and sprightly flow of small talk, but it was uphill work.
Mrs. Maxwell just didn't talk. She reminded Mrs. Cugat of
the female singer in a dance band who sits, wooden and lovely,
staring out over the dancers until it's her turn again. Only it
never seemed to be Mrs. Maxwell's turn. Mr. Cugat was little
help either; he seemed to have caught some of this beautiful
aloofness. Sitting between the two of them, Mrs. Cugat felt
like a twittering sparrow. When they drove up to the small
stucco domicile of Mrs. Maxwell's Aunt Elvie, however, she
was mercifully relieved. Aunt Elvie stuck her head into the
car window and in a breathless spate of words explained that
she was locked out. What she'd done with her key, she
couldn't think. Sometimes she put it under the mat, sometimes in the mailbox — she never carried it, being such a
flibbertigibbet — but it was neither in the mailbox nor under
the mat now — Could someone have stolen it? Did Mr.
Cugat think it was safe to go in? She'd been waiting there on
the steps for Lala for hours, it seemed. 'Why don't all of you
come in and have a drink?' she cried. 'I sure need one!'

'Please do,' said Lala, putting two whole words together in a
lovely contralto, and so, in they went. Another drink was the
last thing on earth Mrs. Cugat needed, but she sipped it

stoically. Mr. Cugat, on his, became, as sometimes happened, charming and slightly old-world.

'I'm so relieved to have Lala running around with nice young married people like you,' confided Aunt Elvie, warming to them both. 'It's an awful responsibility trying to look after her for Melvin. Not that Lala ever does a wrong thing, but the men are just crazy about her, aren't they, honey? And Melvin's so jealous he doesn't want me to let her out of my sight. Lord! I'll never forget the day he came home from Chicago and found that little Mr. Gonzales teaching her to swim. He nearly wiped the floor with him. We had to call in a physician. Melvin's in the marines now, of course,' she added. 'New Guinea.'

Mr. Cugat here, Mrs. Cugat perceived, looked decidedly relieved.

Feeling none too well, she was still lingering over the breakfast table the next morning when Cory sauntered in from the pantry. 'Hello, Beautiful,' he said, patting the top of her head, 'George gone?' Mrs. Cugat nodded.

'Where'd you come from?' she asked testily. 'Did you sleep in the garage again?'

'Tut,' said Private Cartwright, 'I went to bed early and was up with the birds. The Army does that for you, you know. I've been out in the kitchen swapping recipes with Vanilla. She gave me one or two excellent pointers on escalloped potatoes.'

'Cory, are you *really* just a cook?' she asked, her eyes softening. 'You'd think, with all the marvellous financial training you've had —'

'*Just* a cook!' he expostulated. 'Child, you never tasted *anything* like my Potage Mongole. One of the officers asked for more! But look,' he said, suddenly sober, 'what about old George?'

Mrs. Cugat's lips tightened. 'Well, what about him?'

135

'Don't be like that,' he pleaded. 'What's he up to with this gorgeous Maxwell dish? It isn't just like him —'

'He isn't up to anything,' Mrs. Cugat laughed wryly, adding, 'that I know of. But he's having the time of his life — thanks to me. Let me tell you.' So she told him.

'Do you mean that Laura — I mean Mrs. Maxwell — really hasn't got a picture of a fish tattooed on her hip?' exclaimed Cory, sounding relieved.

'No, silly,' she assured him. 'Outside of a dream, whoever heard of such a thing!'

'And the old airedale is just strutting around making like a tiger, with you to blame for it —' Cory murmured. 'It's a nice set-up.'

'It certainly is,' said Mrs. Cugat bitterly, 'and there's not a thing I can do about it.'

'Poor Liz,' he comforted her. 'You always did talk too much.'

She threw a muffin at him and he departed through the window.

'Fool,' she sputtered, but she felt better. She could always count on Cory for support.

As the days went by, however, she began to wonder. The immediate consequence of her taking him into her confidence was the delivery that night, in the middle of a sedate family dinner, of a large and unexpurgated-looking volume entitled *The Ancient Art of Tattooing — Religious and Erotic Significances*. Mrs. Cugat's mother and Mr. Cugat's Aunt Edith were instantly agape.

'Just some little joke between Liz and Cory, I guess,' explained Mr. Cugat blandly. 'Always up to something, those two.'

'We're just a panic, Cory and me,' muttered Mrs. Cugat dourly.

And then, two days later, at a large luncheon given by the

Club Directors for War Bond Committee members, a bellboy interrupted proceedings to ask that Mr. Cugat come to the pool as soon as convenient, as Mrs. Maxwell's water-wings had sprung a leak. Mr. Cugat bore this, too, with equanimity.

Cory also took to addressing Mr. Cugat exclusively as 'Swifty.' Couldn't he see, Mrs. Cugat thought bitterly, that Mr. Cugat liked it. A great help Cory was! A fine friend!

But more serious aspects soon engaged her. Changing one afternoon in the locker-room, she was horrified to hear from the next cubicle an unknown voice hiss breathlessly, 'And, my dear, she's *tattooed* — actually! Her family were side-show people, they say —' Mrs. Cugat stepped quickly outside to protest. 'His poor little wife,' murmured another. 'Does she know?' Mrs. Cugat stepped back in again.

That night she awaited Mr. Cugat with fire in her eye. 'Look,' she said, with deadly calm, confronting him on the doorstep, 'it was bad enough being kidded by friends about our Lala, but this is a little different.'

'What is?' he said wearily, coming into the hall, dropping his briefcase and slinging his panama, with deadly aim, onto the newel post.

Irately, she related her gossip. 'You've just got to put a stop to it,' she fumed.

Mr. Cugat's face hardened. 'I didn't start it, you know,' he said briefly. Then, more sympathetically, he added, 'Good Lord, honey, you're not letting that kind of silly talk get you down, are you? I thought you had more sense. Stir up a cocktail, will you? I crawled home on my eyebrows.' But later that evening this princely unconcern was to desert him.

There was a dance that night at the Club, it being Saturday, and after dinner the usual discussion as to whether they should go, or not, ensued. Only tonight it was Mr. Cugat who was for, and Mrs. Cugat who was against, it — an unusual reversal of sides. Mr. Cugat said he hadn't seen Cory for a couple of days and there were a few things he wanted to discuss with him before he left. Mrs. Cugat didn't care about it at all, but she knew how Mr. Cugat was feeling about losing Cory. The few things he wanted to discuss with him were probably the relative merits of the Cardinals and the Browns which would take place and continue late behind the closed doors of the men's bar where she couldn't get in to break it up, but it would probably be a long time before they'd spend another Saturday night in there together. She could probably find a bridge game.

They walked over, skirting the tenth green, but Mrs. Cugat let this lately significant landmark pass without comment, hoping fervently that she'd never have to see or hear of Mrs. Maxwell and her tattoo again. In this, however, she was disappointed. Stepping through the French doors from the porch into the dining-room, they came in behind four ladies who had drawn up chairs to watch the dancing.

'Her name's MAXWELL,' one was shouting hardily over the blare of the music, 'she teaches SWIMMING.' Mrs. Maxwell, smiling composedly, danced by in the arms of a white-thatched, bantam-sized septuagenarian, who waved gaily and put in a few fancy steps. 'Swimming, did you say? (Look at that old fool!) Why, I had it straight from Lotta Delaplane that she came here with Barnum and Bailey — an acrobat or something —' 'Not really!' 'Well, I hope I'm as democratic as the next, but *after all* —' 'She's a pretty girl — I suppose as long as she's behaving herself —' 'That's just it — she isn't!' Simultaneously the four chairs scraped close and the four heads bent eagerly. '— making a brazen play for young Cugat!' 'Who?' 'Letty Elliot's son-in-law.' 'My dear, NO!' 'How distressing!' 'Poor *Letty!*'

Mrs. Cugat glanced quickly at Mr. Cugat. His jaw was stuck out, his mouth was set, his eyes were steely. Well! she

thought, gratified. Now maybe he'd realize a little what was
going on and take steps to stop it. What Mr. Cugat did was
to drop his arms, which had been folded tensely, step out from
behind the group of chairs, politely begging their occupants'
pardons, and stride out onto the dance floor, where he master-
fully cut in on Mrs. Maxwell. The ladies gaped and Mrs.
Cugat backed hastily out through the French doors. Standing
there in the dark, she watched miserably. So that was how it
was. It was perfectly all right that she be humiliated by gossip — he wouldn't lift a finger — but let him just overhear one
little word against his Laura and he rushed to her rescue like
a knight. Her eyes followed their slowly revolving figures.
Mr. Cugat was looking down into Mrs. Maxwell's upturned
eyes and murmuring in a rather special way he had. She
hadn't seen him do it in years. Her knees felt weak. The
music stopped and they sauntered out into the night through
a door on the other side of the room. Bolstered by pride alone,
she stepped back through the window and doggedly began
trying to get up her bridge game. But she had no success, and
so, after letting pass what she considered enough time to
denote unconcern, she went out onto the grill-room porch
through the same door that Mr. Cugat and Mrs. Maxwell had
used. Mr. Cugat and Mrs. Maxwell and Cory were sitting
there at a small table drinking highballs. Mrs. Maxwell, cool
and silent, Mr. Cugat and Cory hotly discussing the Boston
Red Sox. Mrs. Cugat, with a grateful smile for Cory, joined
them. She watched Mr. Cugat furtively, but his manner with
Mrs. Maxwell was once more impersonal. Cory's, of course,
was nothing short of ardent — but that was always to be expected.

Mr. Cugat was rather silent on the way home. 'What are
you thinking about?' she asked.

'Laura Maxwell,' he replied promptly, and her heart turned
over. 'It's a damned shame to let a lot of fool stories get

started about a perfectly nice girl like that,' he said disgustedly. 'You ought to try and do something about it.'

'Me?'

'Yes, you. You started the whole thing and I should think you'd feel pretty guilty. Poor girl,' he went on, 'new in town and everything. It must be a little hard on her.'

Mrs. Cugat went to bed depressed.

'George must have done a nice job when he taught our Laura to swim,' observed Evie Sturm, coming out of the bath-house onto the gallery that overlooked the pool. Mrs. Cugat's luncheon club were assembled there, sewing for Red Cross. Several pairs of eyes were lifted questioningly. 'I've just been going over the Swimming Meet entries in there,' Mrs. Sturm explained, 'and Mrs. M. is signed up for about five events — including a special diving exhibition all her own.'

'Did George *really* teach Mrs. Maxwell to swim, Liz?' asked Caroline Blake seriously.

'Of course he didn't,' expostulated Mrs. Cugat. 'Thank Heaven this has finally come up while I've got everybody here together. George hardly knew Laura Maxwell, but he had a crazy dream about her wearing a green bathing-suit and being tattooed with a fish and asking him to give her swimming lessons — you know how weird dreams can be — and I couldn't resist teasing him about it. Only before I could stop it, the story ran away with itself and now everybody in town believes it's true. Poor Laura,' she added contritely, 'I feel terribly guilty.'

'You mean she hasn't got a fish tattooed on her hip?' exclaimed somebody, disappointedly.

'Certainly not,' snapped Mrs. Cugat.

'George didn't see it?'

'Of course George didn't see it — he just dreamt it.'

'You're sure?' asked Mrs. Sturm lightly.

'Evie, you make me sick,' sputtered Mrs. Cugat. 'Of course, I'm sure. Whoever heard of such a thing?'

'I can hardly wait to see for myself,' murmured Mrs. Sturm.

The Swimming Meet was the final event of the Country Club season — an event, Mrs. Cugat felt, that she could cheerfully forego. She was getting sicker and sicker of the Country Club. But Mr. Cugat was on the committee and her absence under the circumstances, she felt, might be commented upon. She got dressed for it listlessly and descended to the front porch to wait for him to bring the car around— after about ten minutes sauntering back to the garage to see what the matter was. She found Mr. Cugat trying to remove, with the aid of hot water, soap, and Vanilla's nail file, a banner-like windshield sticker saying, 'Tell It To The Marines.' Cory again, of course. They drove over stiffly.

The pool, bathed in flood lights, was surrounded by flag-draped tiers of seats. The price of admission was a war bond and there was a band and little boys selling popcorn and cokes — and little girls selling cigarettes and programs — and men from *The Chronicle*, *The Spy*, and *The Record* taking people's pictures. Mr. Cugat and somebody else, looking very official in white flannels, bow ties, and no coats, went into a huddle at the springboard. Mrs. Cugat found a seat over near the end. Cory, the Sturms, the Blakes, and Mrs. Maxwell (enveloped in a robe of white towelling) were in a section directly across from her. They waved and beckoned, but she shook her head and remained where she was — in no mood, somehow, for company. Mr. Cugat was now busy lining up eight quivering infants for the first event.

'Who is this Mrs. Maxwell?' asked someone in the row behind Mrs. Cugat. 'It says here "former Aquacade star and holder of the California back stroke record."' Mrs. Cugat hastily consulted her program. Sure enough! Well, she thought relievedly, that ought to help spike a few more rumors about Mr. Cugat and his swimming lessons. Mr. Cugat fired his gun and the infants tumbled into the water and started splashing energetically down the length.

Several events passed, the children getting progressively bigger, more adept, and less entertaining. Mrs. Cugat yawned and decided to go over and join the others, after all. Mrs. Maxwell was now walking, still wrapped in her robe, toward the springboard. The announcer stepped to the microphone. 'Ladies and gentlemen,' he said, 'this next event will be an exhibition of diving by Mrs. Laura Maxwell, one of the country's leading aquatic stars. Later this evening, Mrs. Maxwell will attempt to break her own backstroke record made at Palm Springs in 1941. Mrs. Maxwell!' he bowed. Mr. Cugat stepped gallantly forward to assist with the white robe. Smilingly, Mrs. Maxwell untied the cord and stepped forth. Her limbs were long and golden, her bathing-suit brief and green — and high on one thigh was tattooed a fair-sized fish.

A little gasp followed by a murmur of admiration rippled over the audience. Mrs. Cugat stared numbly. Mr. Cugat's expression was enigmatical. Her eyes sought the other side of the pool. Evie and Howie and the Blakes were grinning with delight. Mrs. Cugat slipped out of her seat and stumbled into the welcoming dark.

Mr. Cugat found her there, huddled in the back seat of the car some three-quarters of an hour later. 'Come on in, I'll buy you a drink,' he offered gently.

'Thank you, no.'

'Hurry up,' he said, opening the car door. Mrs. Cugat got out.

'There now, that's better, isn't it?' he asked, leaning against

142

the bar at her side and watching while she silently sipped a highball. Tears, maddeningly, welled up. Mr. Cugat ignored them.

'There's something very funny about that tattoo,' he remarked.

'There certainly is!' she managed.

'Do you suppose I'm getting psychic or something?' he asked solemnly. Mrs. Cugat gave him a withering look. Another tear splashed down. 'I didn't know she had one — honest,' he said.

Mrs. Cugat turned to look at him. 'Didn't you — *really?*' she gulped.

The door of the bar burst open. Cory and a radiant Mrs. Maxwell swung in. 'She did it!' he crowed, beaming idiotically.

Mr. and Mrs. Cugat turned. 'What?' they asked blankly.

'She broke her own record! Man-oh-man, what a mermaid! Say, you two, how about —' he paused suddenly, and then blurted, 'What's the matter with Liz?' Mrs. Cugat averted her head. 'Child, child, you aren't crying, are you? Holy Mike!' he exclaimed suddenly, '*the tattoo!* Sweetheart, show 'em!' Mrs. Maxwell obligingly stuck out a golden leg. The fish was still there, but only faintly discernible. 'Liz, honey,' he apologized, 'I never meant *you* to fall for it. I bribed Laura to let me draw it on with a fountain pen, just to give old George a scare. I thought you'd be sitting with us and I could tip you off. But I got so excited watching the exhibition that I forgot all about it. Did you ever see such a stroke? It's perfect! Or nearly — there's one little thing, Baby —'

'There is?' Mrs. Maxwell smiled up at him. 'Will you show me?' she asked softly.

'Will I!'

Mr. and Mrs. Cugat turned back to the bar and leaned

there, shoulders touching. 'Well,' she smiled, lifting her glass, 'pleasant dreams!'

Mr. Cugat's eyes softened and he leaned forward and dropped a kiss on her tear-stained cheek. Then he raised his eyes. Mrs. Cugat turned. The biggest marine she had ever seen was coming through the door.

'Could you tell me if Mrs. Melvin Maxwell is here tonight?' he inquired of the bartender gruffly. 'I'm her husband — Captain Maxwell.'

Mr. Cugat put down his drink. 'Mrs. Maxwell just went down to the pool with Private Cartwright,' he said pleasantly. 'He's teaching her to swim. Can I — show you the way?'

10

TAKING A NAME IN VAIN

Dᴀᴍᴇ Nᴀᴛᴜʀᴇ, having been undeniably dilatory in the matter of seeing to the prolongation of the Cugat line, bethought herself one fine day and, contrite, arranged for twins. Mrs. Cugat came home from Doctor MacHarg's office, on the afternoon that he confirmed his suspicions of these profuse amends, beaming with pride.

'Is he *sure?*' queried Mr. Cugat, aghast.

'Positive,' she replied happily. 'Here's a picture he took. I asked him if I might keep it.'

'Darling,' chattered Mr. Cugat, 'you shouldn't be looking at things like that!' He snatched the X-ray print hastily from her and regarded it bug-eyed.

'I don't know why not, silly,' said Mrs. Cugat. 'Our own children!' She bent tenderly over the print and then gently took it from Mr. Cugat's flabby grasp and turned it the other way up. Mr. Cugat, somewhat white, regarded this misty preview of his progeny dazedly for about five minutes and then got up and went out for a drink. Mrs. Cugat, humming happily, propped the print on her dressing-table and went to phone her mother.

Her mother, naturally, came right over, and Mr. Cugat, in an illogical panic, fled to the pantry, from whence he was rescued, half an hour later, in pathetic condition, due to hav-

ing mistakenly confided in Vanilla, who had, it appeared, at
one time, been a midwife.

Soothed and comforted, at length, he was prevailed upon to
take courage and have some dinner, but he sat nervously
crumbling his bread throughout most of the meal and listened
to their dauntless chatter lost in wonder.

They talked vivaciously — of bassinettes — of baby buggies
— of christening robes — of names. The bassinette which had
held the infant Mrs. Cugat and which, retrimmed with fresh
point d'esprit, they had been expecting to use, would not, it
seemed, do now. Two new bassinettes exactly alike would
have to be ordered. One pink, one blue. They discussed
the practicality of switching the trimming from point d'esprit
to pleated organza. The English pram, which had been
promised by an obliging young aunt, incautiously protesting
that she had no further use for it, was likewise out. And it
would, of course, be next to impossible to borrow a twin buggy
— that, too, would have to be ordered. And *two* christening
robes! And two high-chairs and twice as many diapers —
binders — and shirts. Having twins, they exclaimed with
enthusiasm, was going to be *twice* as expensive!

'Almost two and three-quarters times,' Mr. Cugat cor-
rected them abstractedly.

They took up the subject of twin names — alphabetically.
Andrew and Anthony and David and Derek and Joel and
Jonathan, in case they were boys; Anne and Amanda and
Candace and Carlotta and Dinah and Deborah, in case they
were girls; Patrick and Patricia and Terence and Tilda and
Simon and Susan, in case there was one of each. They consulted Mr. Cugat eagerly and urged him to express an opinion
or offer a suggestion, but he just said, nervously toying with
his dessert, that he'd rather wait and see, and then watched,
awed, while Mrs. Cugat finished off, with gusto, her third dish
of rice pudding.

Three months went by during which time Mrs. Cugat set-tled confidently on Anne and Amanda, knitted assiduously, ate a great deal more rice pudding, and put up with Mr. Cugat, who seemed singularly impelled to oscillate between smother-ing devotion and unwonted dissipation. That is, on one night he'd keep her wearily sitting on the sidelines at a Club dance while he sought alleviation from anxiety in the men's bar and the very next night drive her nearly wild by helplessly hover-ing with unnecessary cushions, footstools, and glasses of milk. However, in time, there comes an end to every ordeal and she joyfully called him at the office one bright spring morning to announce that she thought the day had arrived.

Mr. Cugat, white-lipped and queerly shy, hastened home and, with shaking hands and his hat still on, attempted to help her pack a bag, but after three times removing a large lace pincushion from it which seemed to persist in coming under his hand, she pushed him gently toward a chair. 'Why don't you just sit here?' she said kindly. 'Let me get you a highball or something —' Thoughtfully, she stepped out into the hall to have her next pain. Kindly persons took him in charge, however, when they reached the hospital and, relieved, she went off to get down to the business at hand.

It was Cory Cartwright, Mr. Cugat's lifelong fair and foul weather friend who, while Mrs. Cugat napped defenseless, took it upon himself to bestow more fitting names upon Anne and Amanda. Their first caller, he took one delighted look at them, displayed behind the plate-glass window of the hospital nursery and ebulliently rechristened them Moe and Joe. Within twelve hours, everybody was calling them Moe and Joe. Mrs. Cugat woke up and tried to protest, but she found herself in a peculiarly bemused state which seemed to render her incapable of much of anything but an ecstatic smile, and Mr. Cugat was still dazed. It seemed sensible just to go on calling them Moe and Joe — until everybody felt a little stronger and more capable of deciding between Andrew and Anthony or David and Derek or Joel and Jonathan.

Mrs. Cugat came home from the hospital, Mr. Cugat returned gradually to normal, and Moe and Joe waxed fat and kicked. Moe and Joe were perfectly charming — utterly indistinguishable one from the other and their fame spread far and wide. Mrs. Cugat maintained stoutly that they weren't one bit alike, but Mr. Cugat could often be noted looking at them with the anxious expression of a man seeing double.

'Their personalities are wholly different,' Mrs. Cugat reiterated one day to her mother as they watched fatuously while Moe waved his arms and Joe waved his legs. 'Moe puts things in his mouth and Joe throws things.'

'Dear,' said Mrs. Cugat's mother, 'don't you think it's time you did something about their names? The bishop was saying only the other day that he supposed the christening would be soon.'

'I know,' said Mrs. Cugat, 'we really must. We keep putting it off. I'll talk to George tonight.'

'And there are the godparents to think of, too,' her mother reminded her.

Mr. Cugat, on being approached that evening, was now found to be surprisingly positive in his views on names. He summarily threw out Andrew and Anthony and David and Derek and Joel and Jonathan as pure whimsy and plumped vigorously for Baldwin C. (after Mrs. Cugat's father) and J. Duncan (after his esteemed employer, Mr. Atterbury). Mrs. Cugat considered these wistfully. They seemed ponderous and unwieldy — not liable to anything very appealing in nicknames, certainly. She'd been particularly fond of David and Derek — Davey and Derry were so cunning. There wasn't much you could call a Duncan but 'Dunc' and simply nothing you could call a Baldwin but 'Baldy'! Still it would be nice to name one after her father. Her mother would like it. Also, Mr. Cugat's mind seemed to be made up.

'We have to think of two godmothers and four godfathers,' she said, sturdily attacking the next problem.

His ideas on this matter, it appeared, were no less clear. 'How about having Mr. Atterbury and Cory for Moe,' he said promptly, 'and Bill Stone and somebody for Joe?' Adding generously, 'You think of the godmothers.'

But Mrs. Cugat was strangling with indignation. 'Bill Stone!' she finally managed to sputter in an outraged voice — 'that *awful* man?'

'Honey,' said Mr. Cugat, smiling patiently, 'he happens to be one of my oldest friends and a better lad, incidentally, never lived. Just because your bridge club doesn't happen to approve of him —'

'Approve of him!' exclaimed Mrs. Cugat. 'That menace! Has he ever drawn a sober breath — or once been seen with anyone respectable?'

Mr. Cugat smiled indulgently. 'You girls don't know a really good guy when you see one, that's all. Just because he lives down at the Club and gets out on the town occasionally —'

'I won't have him!' she declared stoutly. 'He's a disgrace!' But Mr. Cugat had got a certain look on his face and she knew she was butting a stone wall. 'Who are you going to have for the other one,' she asked sourly, 'the bartender down at Eddie's?'

Mr. Cugat ignored this sally. 'Well,' he said, after a little thought, 'how about Professor McCracken? He was awfully good to me when I was a kid at the Academy and I know it would please him.'

Mrs. Cugat thought this over. 'But George,' she protested, 'that gives Moe, Mr. Atterbury — who will probably crash through with something very handsome, and Cory — who'd give anybody the shirt off his back — and poor little Joe nobody but that rip, Bill Stone, and old Professor McCracken, who hasn't a cent to his name. It isn't fair. We've got to think of somebody — substantial — for Joe, too, so he'll get nice presents.'

Mr. Cugat was shocked. 'You do that,' he said, with disgust, 'and you'll end up with somebody so far-fetched that they can't possibly miss what they were asked for!'

'I know,' admitted Mrs. Cugat, 'but everybody does it. Look at the *Simpsons* having *Howie Sturm!* Blatant!'

'A lot of good it ever does,' grumbled Mr. Cugat; 'I don't think my godparents know I'm alive — and where have yours been keeping themselves?'

'One of my godmothers gave me a little ermine muff once,' she said absently. Then her face cleared. 'I know,' she cried, 'Uncle Simpson!'

'And who is Uncle Simpson?' asked Mr. Cugat blankly.

'Well, he's my father's oldest brother. He lives up in Ridgeway in the old house where they were all born and he's simply wading in money. He's quite old and a little peculiar — he doesn't speak to some of the family — but Mother said he sent a nice basket to Daddy's funeral — she was quite surprised at the time — so he must like us.'

'That was fifteen years ago,' put in Mr. Cugat. 'Has anybody seen or heard of him since?'

'Mother hasn't, I don't believe — he doesn't get out much. But he must know about the twins — everybody knows about the twins.' Mr. Cugat looked doubtful. 'Why, he's just the one!' she went on, rapidly selling herself the idea. 'He's the head of the family and, since Daddy's dead, it's very suitable. He'll probably be terribly pleased. I expect he's really very nice if you're just nice to him. The others probably try to get something out of him all the time.' Mr. Cugat snorted, but she ignored it. 'If I give in and let you have that horrible Bill Stone,' she asserted — 'and I don't know how I'll stand it but I suppose I'll have to — the least you can do is let me have my own uncle. After all, the twins are half mine, you know, and I went to a good deal of trouble to get them.' Mr. Cugat, suddenly meek, admitted this was so and she hurried upstairs to write the letter.

Somewhat to everybody's surprise, Uncle Simpson wrote, in a gouty hand, on yellowed paper, embellished with a forgotten coat-of-arms, that he supposed it was up to him to come — although he was far from well — and that he would arrive the Saturday evening before the ceremony. It was arranged that Mrs. Cugat's mother have him at her house — Moe and Joe, with their appurtenances, having taken over the guest-room, and Miss Brownlow, the trained nurse — staying until Mrs. Cugat was stronger — being in possession of the back bedroom.

The bishop came to call and Moe and Joe showed off to advantage — so engagingly, in fact, that he offered to officiate himself. Mr. Atterbury professed himself delighted at the honor bestowed upon him and crashed through even more handsomely than anticipated — with shares of Tri-State Bank stock. Uncle Simpson's arrival was nervously awaited.

He arrived, as promised, on Saturday evening, and after dinner, later reported by Mrs. Cugat's mother to have consisted of two crackers made of seaweed and a glass of water, was brought over to view his godchild. Mrs. Cugat realized when he walked in the door that she had never been quite so frightened of anybody before. He looked like an aged lizard and appeared to be in such an advanced state of boredom that a mere civil handshake cost him effort. Mr. Cugat hurried forward to help him with his coat, but was brushed off.

'Can I take your hat?' he ventured timidly. But Uncle

Simpson chose to retain this also. He came into the living-room, gave one sharp look around, and then lapsed again into long-suffering.

'The twins are in the nursery,' said Mrs. Cugat nervously, 'but I can have them brought down —'

'Either way, either way,' he murmured impatiently.

'We'll go up, of course,' put in Mrs. Cugat's mother in a light, firm voice.

'This is Miss Brownlow,' said Mrs. Cugat at the nursery door, and Miss Brownlow, all unwarned, bustled forward with a sparkling smile, said, 'We've got something pretty nice to show you, Mr. — I-didn't-quite-catch-the-name?' and was withered by a look.

'Which one?' growled Uncle Simpson, advancing upon the bassinettes. Mrs. Cugat pointed mutely to Joe's blue organza nest. Walking straight past the pink bassinette without a glance, he peered intently down on the sleeping Joe. Joe opened his eyes, crossed them, and threw up.

Uncle Simpson turned away. 'He looks nothing whatever like any of us,' he said, giving Mr. Cugat a cursory glance and made for the door.

'Oh, Mother and I think sometimes (don't we, Mother?) that when he sits up — you can tell better then — that he's going to be the image of Daddy,' interpolated Mrs. Cugat anxiously.

'That would be a pity,' said Uncle Simpson dryly, 'Baldy had a weak face.'

He departed soon after, observing that the house seemed unnecessarily large for young people and must be expensive to run, and Mr. and Mrs. Cugat, closing the door, fell shattered into each other's arms. 'Poor little Joe,' she mourned. 'Oh, why did he have to spit up? — he hardly ever does.'

'Neither do I,' said Mr. Cugat tersely, 'but I came damned close to it.'

The christening was at four the following afternoon and the assemblage that gathered in the chapel of Saint Jude's was select and fashionable. Moe and Joe, under their robes of lawn and lace, kicked in vain and grew red in the face and Mr. and Mrs. Cugat, in the first pew, dandled them nervously while Miss Brownlow, with a ready handkerchief, kept her eye on Joe. Behind them, Mr. Atterbury beamed, pink and benevolent, and Mrs. Atterbury, in white orchids, whispered vivaciously to Mr. Cugat's little Aunt Edith, Moe's godmother-to-be. Cory and Bill Stone sat stiffly, resplendent in their uniforms, and across the aisle, Joe's godmother-to-be, Mrs. Cugat's Cousin Melba from Cincinnati, stared at Mr. Stone's quarter profile, frankly intrigued. Beside Mrs. Cugat's mother, who looked as if she'd had about all of him she could take, Uncle Simpson sat with folded arms, staring stonily at the ceiling.

The bishop appeared, the humming of the organ died away, and Mrs. Cugat and Moe and his sponsors took their places. Moe cooed and gurgled and waved his arms and then fell into a convenient trance, eyes fastened on a candle flame. At the charge, 'Name this child,' Mr. Atterbury hurrumped and spoke up proudly, 'James Duncan,' and the bishop's voice repeated sonorously, 'James Duncan, I baptize thee in the name of the Father and of the Son and of the Holy Ghost. Amen.' Somewhat weak-kneed, Mrs. Cugat, bearing the regenerated Moe, returned to her place.

Then Mr. Cugat and Joe, Uncle Simpson, Bill Stone, and Cousin Melba took their places — Mr. Cugat hunched and rigid with Joe propped high on one shoulder. Joe humped his back like a caterpillar, tried to put Mr. Cugat's ear in his mouth, and chortled gleefully and the back of Mr. Cugat's neck turned from pink to red. Darling little Joe, thought Mrs. Cugat, watching apprehensively — one more hump and he'd be over Mr. Cugat's shoulder and onto the floor. Her eyes went to the group about him. Really! Poor innocent. Here was Moe, secure and dozing in her arms, sponsored by the very nicest people and little Joe up there being handed Uncle Simpson, Bill Stone, and Cousin Melba. Uncle Simpson now had his hands clasped under his coat tails and his head thrust forward and was giving the fish-eye to the bishop. Bill Stone looked solemn and appeared to be actually listening to what was being said. Never heard it before, probably! Cousin Melba was still looking at Bill Stone. Cousin Melba was a dear, but man-crazy. Always had been. Anything in pants. Look at her! Although Mrs. Cugat had to admit that the current Bill Stone, who had flown in only that morning from a Southern hospital, was, with all those wings and ribbons and that limp, rather impressive.

'Name this child,' adjured the bishop again.

'Ulysses Simpson,' cracked Uncle Simpson like the shot out of a pistol.

Mrs. Cugat caught her breath and Mr. Cugat started and halfway turned. Little Doctor Bennett, at the bishop's side, looked up questioningly.

'Ulysses Simpson,' intoned the Bishop, 'I baptize thee in the name of the Father and of the Son and of the Holy Ghost. Amen.'

Joe stiffened and threw up.

'That horrible old man!' gasped Mrs. Cugat, on their way home in the car. 'That was no misunderstanding! He knew perfectly well we were naming Joe after Daddy. He did it on purpose.'

'Well, he *might* not have,' said Mr. Cugat placatingly. 'You know — he's old, and the fact that Mr. Atterbury's godson was being named after him may have got him confused and he thought —'

'Any time that old rhinoceros gets confused, I want to be

there to see it!' sputtered Mrs. Cugat. 'Wishing a name like Ulysses on darling little Joe! He's going to have to do something pretty big to make up for it, I can tell you!' She paused thoughtfully. 'What do you suppose he is planning to do about Joe, anyway? He couldn't be so inhuman and ungrateful and bad-mannered as just to ignore him, could he?'

'Nothing would surprise me,' said Mr. Cugat.

But Uncle Simpson had not forgotten his namesake. Arriving home, they found him waiting in his overcoat in the front hall — Mrs. Cugat's mother and Aunt Edith and Mrs. Atterbury doing all in their power to prevail upon him to stay with the rest and have some champagne. He held in his hand a small and ancient leather case.

'This is for my godson,' he said curtly, giving it to Mrs. Cugat — 'your grandfather's stick-pin.'

'Why, how nice!' exclaimed Mrs. Cugat gamely. 'Is it a garnet?' It was.

'Everything else, you may or *may not* know,' went on Uncle Simpson, 'I'm leaving to the church. God knows I'm not a religious man, but I don't intend to let the Democrats have it to spend!' Whereupon, he shook hands briefly, clapped on his hat, was boosted into a Peerless limousine and departed.

The christening party progressed much as such parties are prone to — a considerable number of mixed relatives being present and all ages represented. Moe and Joe were admired, cooed at and discussed, and Moe put things in his mouth and Joe, unaware of the slump his prospects had taken, profligately threw things around. Mrs. Cugat, covering indignant disappointment with a bright smile, moved from group to group and wished she could sit down. Mr. Cugat, the begetter of twins, wore his laurels with becoming modesty and deftly parried banter. Mr. Atterbury made quite a long speech. Bill Stone, on whom Mrs. Cugat was keeping a sharp eye, continued exemplary and solemn, drinking but one glass of champagne and bending a polite ear to Cousin Melba — although Cory, Mrs. Cugat suspected, in another half hour would be doing his imitations. Really, if she couldn't sit down somewhere for just a minute in peace and quiet (how pleasant the hospital had been!) she'd fall down. She slipped out into the pantry and was just about to sink down to the bottom step of a step-ladder there when she discovered that she had been followed by Mr. Stone. He came in hesitantly, looking acutely embarrassed. Mrs. Cugat tried to cover her irritation.

'I want to leave this for Joe,' he said, taking an envelope out of his pocket and laying it on the sink. Then he cleared his throat. 'You know, I've never been a godfather before — but I'll try to make a good one.'

Mrs. Cugat reddened and laughed a little embarrassedly. 'I'm sure you will, Bill,' she said, as kindly as she could, and then added awkwardly, 'It was terribly nice of you to come all that way just for the ceremony — we did appreciate it — Oh, dear, I'm afraid people are leaving — thank you, again, so much — I'd better get back — you're going to be here for a while, aren't you?'

Mr. Stone stood still, looking down at her. 'No,' he said, smiling, 'so, good-bye. Take good care of him, won't you?'

When she remembered the envelope again, Mr. Cugat was emerging from the pantry with it two hours later. 'Where'd this come from?' he asked in a funny voice.

Mrs. Cugat, sitting cross-legged on the hearth between Moe and Joe on their blankets, stared up at him blankly. 'Oh!' she said finally, 'Bill Stone left it — I forgot.'

'Good God!'

'Why? What is it?'

'It's his will.'

'His *will!*'

'Yes,' said Mr. Cugat, his voice now definitely strange. 'He's

156

going back to the Pacific, you know — in spite of all he's had
— but he doesn't care, I guess — he's all alone.'

'But why did he leave it here?   He said it was something for
— Oh!'

Mr. Cugat nodded and swallowed.

'Little Joe, right now, looks like being a millionaire.'

'Oh — G-George!' she stammered, her eyes stinging, 'Bill
— *can't* do that!'

'No.'

There was a sharp ping on one of the andirons, followed by
a little jet of sparks. Ulysses Simpson Cugat had thrown
Grandpa's garnet in the fire.

THE END